AIRY ALLIES AND ENEMIES

A RAINA SUN MYSTERY

ANNE R. TAN

To Sven,
not the reindeer in Frozen

1

FREE LUNCH

In the audience, Raina Sun Louie watched in horror as her grandma's coconut bra fell onto the open-air stage. Her grandma continued to gyrate the grass skirt and flung her arms about in the Hawaiian dance. The flickering tiki torches and spotlight followed her every move. Knowing her grandma, Po Po probably had on a beige-colored tank top, but to the audience at the luau, she looked topless.

The other four couples at the table gasped at the performance. This probably wasn't the dinner show they thought they paid for. Raina glanced around the outdoor dining patio. Everyone in the audience was staring at the stage with equal parts curiosity and disbelief.

Next to Raina, her husband, Matthew Louie, coughed and squirted the Mai Tai drink out of his nose. "Oh, sh—"

"No, no, no," Raina cut in, shaking her head in disbelief. "We're on our honeymoon. Po Po is not here. That's not her. All little old Chinese grannies look the same."

On stage, a shirtless young Asian man in a grass skirt danced over to the coconut bra, flipped it up in the air with his foot, and caught it in one hand with a flourish. Still gyrating his hip, the man whirled around Po Po and tied on the bra.

"And that's your brother, Winter Sun," Matthew said, setting his glass down with a thud on the table.

Raina closed her eyes and rubbed her temples. Why were her grandma and baby brother in Kauai? Didn't they understand a honeymoon meant alone time with her husband? It was bad enough the humidity had turned her curly black hair into a cotton candy puff, but uninvited family members at her honeymoon? No, this was not happening. Not on her watch.

She opened her eyes and threw her napkin onto the table. "Let's go. If we duck out of here now, we can avoid them. Then we're flying to another island. They can't do this to me."

Matthew shook his head and pointed to the stage. "Too late."

On stage, Po Po held a microphone and waved in the Louies' direction. "Yoo-hoo! Love birds! We have a surprise for you, Rainy."

The other four couples at the table swiveled their

heads to stare at the Louies. Raina slid an inch lower in her seat and avoided eye contact.

Matthew chuckled. "I knew a free trip was too good to be true."

Raina smacked her husband's forearm. If only a hole would open in the ground. She would gladly jump in it. "Seriously? You think this is funny?" she whispered.

"This morning, you were complaining about the slow pace around here," Matthew whispered back. His gold-flecked brown eyes twinkled with laughter. He pointed at the evening sky. "The ancestors are listening."

The cool breeze shifted, and Raina smelled her husband's sage and clean water scent, a tantalizing combination from his hair product, soap, and after-shave. "This is all your fault. We've been here three days, and this is our third luau."

"What man can turn down meat cooked in a sand-pit? Besides"—Matthew held up his right wrist to show off the black wristband—"we can't turn down a free dinner show. Everyone else has to pay a hundred bucks to be here. We have gotten six hundred dollars' worth of food and entertainment."

The black wristband from the resort gave them VIP access to the nightly dinner show, and Matthew intended to take full advantage of this perk. Her husband's Chinese frugality had gotten them into trouble before, like when they purchased a foreclosed house with a body in the wall.

"If we had gone somewhere else for dinner, my grandma wouldn't have been able to track us down," Raina said. She sounded like a petulant child, but this was her belated honeymoon. After a yearlong home remodel and a stressful new job, she deserved a vacation. A real vacation—where there were no dead bodies and kooky relatives.

Matthew shrugged. "Hey, I'm Chinese. Frugality is in my blood."

Raina harrumphed and crossed her arms. She might have turned out the same if her family had lost all their wealth in the dot-com bust like his family. And her husband's frugality was also wrapped up in his hang-up about being the provider. Asian males. They were a different beast.

On stage, the Hawaiian dancers finished their act. Po Po and Win gave the Louies one final wave and exited. The emcee appeared and introduced the next act.

"Let's go back to our room and bar the door," Raina said. "They will come looking for us any minute now."

Matthew glanced at a spot over Raina's shoulder. "Too late." He shoved another bite of the kalua pork into his mouth. He probably wanted to get as much food in his stomach before their dinner got interrupted further.

Raina glanced over her shoulder. Her eyes widened

at the sight of her grandma, baby brother, and a Polynesian woman in a muumuu dress making a beeline toward her table. She jerked up, knocking over her chair. "If you love me, you will stall them." She took off for their hotel room, her flip-flop sandals slapping against her feet.

"Yoo-hoo! Rainy! I gotta business proposition for you," Po Po called out. Since her grandma was a regular at the senior exercise classes, she had no problem keeping up with Raina.

"I don't know you, you crazy old coot," Raina shouted back. A small flash of amusement shot through her. She had always wanted to call her grandma an old coot. She wasn't sure why she put up this show of resistance and prolonged this embarrassing trek across the beach toward the resort. Maybe she had also inherited some of her grandma's love for theatrics.

Her foot slipped off the foam flip-flop, and Raina crashed headfirst onto the sand. Great. She lay on the warm sand for a long moment, waiting for her heart rate to calm down. Her husband belly laughed in the background. She spat out sand from her mouth. Her tongue traced her teeth, dislodging the remaining grit, and she spat again. The corners of her mouth twitched, but she forced her smile away. It would only encourage her grandma.

Footsteps approached Raina. Someone grabbed Raina's arm and hauled her into a sitting position.

Po Po squatted down until she was face-to-face with Raina. In Chinese, Po Po was the formal title for a maternal grandmother and also a term of respect for elderly ladies. Her legal name was Bonnie Wong.

Her grandma's silvery-white hair had grown from a pixie cut to a shaggy bob with bangs that highlighted her warm, brown eyes. Though barely over five feet tall, Po Po wasn't someone who understood "no" or "later," much like a toddler.

"I don't know why you ran, but we both know you can't escape me," Po Po said. Her grandma's other favorite word was "mine" when it came to family. There was no fleeing the matriarch of the Wong family. Once you were in, it was for life.

"I have to try," Raina said in a pretend stern voice. "I can't just roll over and let you walk all over me."

Po Po gave Raina a deadpan stare. "I can see how a faceplant would be more appealing."

Raina shifted her gaze to her brother. "I blame you for this fiasco. I will remember this, buddy. Some day, I will have my vengeance."

Win held up both hands and gave her a cheeky grin. "She would have come with or without me. I'm just here for the beach and girls in bikinis."

Raina rolled her eyes. Trust a twenty-one-year-old to focus on the important things in life.

Win had grown since the last time she saw him, filling out so that he looked more like an adult than a man-child. All traces of his former geeky high school years were gone. Instead, he appeared to be going for the beach bum look with his black hair in a man bun, and his face looked scruffy, like he was failing at growing a beard. Raina much preferred her husband's close-cropped black hair, a remnant from his Marine days. Both men were of the same height, with a runner's physique and appetite.

Matthew sauntered over and stood next to Win, rubbing his stomach. "I don't know what's in the pork, but I can eat it at every meal." He stifled a burp. "Are we having the powwow right here? Or do we need more privacy?"

Her stoic husband had changed since their marriage, but this was the first time she saw him this relaxed in front of strangers. Normally, his piercing cop eyes roamed the scene, evaluating its hidden threat. Maybe there was something in the pork. Or maybe it was the free Mai Tai drinks.

"Auntie May needs a small favor," Po Po said. "Her family owns the resort and gave us a good discount for your stay." She arched an eyebrow, asking if Raina understood her obligation for the family discount.

Raina sighed inwardly. Auntie May was married to her grandpa's older brother. During Raina's childhood, she had met Auntie May a few times when her great-aunt visited San Francisco. Why did free always come with hidden strings? The six hundred dollars' worth of free food and entertainment that her husband had bragged about a few minutes earlier now felt cheap in comparison. She gave her grandma a slight nod. Oh, she understood the hidden obligation behind the family discount all right.

Po Po gestured at the woman in the muumuu dress standing next to her. "This is Leilani Wong, Auntie May's granddaughter and your second cousin."

The last time Raina had seen her cousin was over a decade ago. "I thought you were on a business trip," Raina said.

"I had to cut it short because a situation came up," Leilani said. "I just got back to the resort this afternoon."

Her cousin was half Polynesian and half Chinese. She was in her late twenties but going on forty. It might be the sun or stress. Raina wasn't a fashionista, but even she knew a bright-red Hawaiian muumuu dress made a stocky figure look even wider. Her cousin's brown eyes were worried, but her smile was welcoming.

"I am so happy to see you again, Sherlock Holmes," Leilani continued. "Your grandma has told me so much about your adventures together."

Raina shifted her gaze to Po Po and back to her cousin. "Don't believe half the stuff that comes out of my grandma's mouth." She raised a hand to her mouth and pretended to whisper. "She reads too many mystery books."

Matthew opened his mouth, but Raina gave him a

pointed look. The smart man promptly closed his mouth and reached down to help Raina off the ground.

Raina brushed the sand off her tank top and shorts. "I am happy to help." And she was. Having grown up in San Francisco, she wasn't used to the slow pace on the island. It had only been three days, and—while she would never admit it out loud—she was slightly bored with relaxing.

"That's great, Rainy, but we need Matthew, too," Po Po said.

"How can I be of service?" Matthew said with a tight smile.

Raina bit the inside of her cheek to keep from laughing. Wasn't gluttony a sin? Now her husband had to work for his free pork.

"I need someone to do a ransom drop," Leilani said. "A few days ago, someone kidnapped my younger sister."

2

RANSOM MONEY

The next day, Raina adjusted her curly, black hair to hide the wireless earpiece. At the kidnapper's request, the ten thousand dollars ransom money was disguised as a package of maxi pads. Each pink wrapper hid a thousand dollars in hundred-dollar bills, folded neatly in half. Raina tucked the package into the waistband of her shorts and covered it with her T-shirt. "I'm ready to rock-and-roll."

Matthew replied in the earpiece, "I'm in place." Her husband was on foot somewhere near the drop-off location, waiting to tail the pick-up person.

In the driver's seat of the minivan, Leilani gave Raina a thumbs up. She wore jeans and a pink button-down shirt. Maybe the muumuus were the uniform she wore for work. Her other hand held Po Po's bird-watching binoculars. "Good luck. I'm ready to pick up Matthew and follow the getaway car."

Not for the first time, Raina wondered why Auntie May didn't want her eldest granddaughter doing the drop-off. Maybe she feared this could be an opportunity for the kidnapper to grab another family member. She hadn't notified the local police. With rumors of corruption and cronyism, Raina understood Auntie May's reluctance. Instead, she had called her sister-in-law, and Po Po and Win booked the first flight out of San Francisco.

Besides, Matthew was a former Marine and currently a homicide detective in their hometown, which was probably more experience than the local cop assigned to the case would have. Raina admitted that she might be slightly biased.

From the passenger seat, Po Po studied her tablet. Her grandma's hacker friend had rerouted the open-air mall's video feed to the tablet. "I don't see anyone suspicious yet. Just regular folks using the bathroom."

Raina wiped her sweaty hands on her baggy shorts, squared her shoulders, and opened the sliding door of the minivan. As she stepped out, a warm blast of air hit her. Her hair instantly recoiled at the humidity and stuck to the back of her neck. She strolled across the parking lot with butterflies in the pit of her stomach and her eyes roaming the scene.

The kidnapper was probably a local who knew the layout of the open-air mall. The middle area was the food court with wood picnic benches, a large canopy for shade, and a stage for entertainment. The potted plants helped create the illusion of an oasis.

Each store was a circular or square hut with a thatch roof. There was some attempt at creating a row of shops, but the huts mostly zigzagged around each other, looking as if the builder had a little too much to drink. Or maybe inefficient shopping was part of the slower pace island charm.

The kidnapper was also smart enough to ask Auntie May to disguise the ransom money. Who would pick up an opened package of maxi pads by the public restroom? Most people couldn't get over the gross factor or the pink color. It was too bad Po Po's hacker friend couldn't trace the kidnapper's phone call.

The restroom building was right next to the parking lot in this part of the mall. It had two entrances, the women on the left and the men on the right. Smack in the middle was a metal trashcan. Raina trotted over, bent down, and wedged the maxi pad package in the gap between the trashcan and the building wall. She stood and turned around to scan the area, looking like she was waiting for someone.

People came and went. No one paid any particular attention to Raina. A young mom with a wide-brim hat pushed a bassinet stroller into the restroom. The black hair that cascaded down her shoulders had white streaks in it. Maybe she was imitating Rogue from the *X-Men*, but the white streaks only made Raina think of Frankenstein's bride. The stroller's shade canopy was up with a blanket thrown over the top to block out the sun. Raina hoped there was enough air circulation for the napping baby. She returned her attention to the parking lot.

The pick-up person probably wouldn't show up until Raina left the area. It wouldn't surprise her if the pick-up person also had access to the video feed. She sauntered to a nearby hut selling souvenirs and loitered in front of the shop windows, half-hidden by a rack of sun hats. She was close enough to see the pick-up, but too far to catch up to the person.

Raina spoke into her smartwatch, a birthday present from her grandma. She had to modulate her tone to keep from sounding too excited. Given the tense situation, it would be awkward if Leilani knew Raina got a dopamine hit from the action. "I delivered the package. Do you see anything, Watson?"

"No one suspicious, Sherlock," Po Po said in the earpiece. She had insisted on code names for Operation Maxi. "I wonder how long we'll have to wait."

"Patience is a virtue in a stakeout," Raina replied.

"This is not a stakeout," Matthew grumbled in the earpiece. "It's an *I Love Lucy* episode."

Raina agreed with her husband's assessment of the situation. She was able to talk her brother out of joining Operation Maxi by asking him to babysit Auntie May. Win had agreed when it meant spending the morning at the beach.

"That mom has been in the restroom for quite a

while. The baby must have had a blowout," Po Po said conversationally.

"Silence is also a virtue in a stakeout," Matthew said.

"We can't just sit here in silence," Po Po said.

"Yes, we can," Matthew said.

Raina sighed. As the director of the senior center, she had to play referee for her grandma daily at work. She didn't expect to play this role while on vacation, too.

The young mom with the baby stroller came out of the restroom and tossed a dirty diaper into the trashcan but missed. She bent down to retrieve the diaper and threw it into the trashcan again. The blanket was still draped over the stroller.

Raina frowned. The young mom must be an old pro at changing diapers without waking the baby.

Footsteps approached from behind Raina. "Excuse me, can I help you with something?" the store clerk asked.

Raina glanced over her shoulder. "Ah, no, thanks. I'm just looking."

The store clerk didn't move. "We have another rack of hats in the back. Is there a particular style you're looking for?"

Raina returned her gaze to the storefront window. The young mom was walking toward Raina's direction, her face half-hidden underneath the shade of the wide-brim hat. "I'll come back," Raina called out over her shoulder to the store clerk.

As Raina power walked out of the store, she spoke into her smartwatch. "Watson, check to see if the maxi pads are still peeking out from behind the trashcan."

For half a second, there was silence on the line. "It's gone," Po Po said through the earpiece. "But I didn't see anyone pick it up."

The young mom was less than five feet away from Raina, her head bowed low. There was something oddly familiar about her posture. She was taller than Raina's five foot three inches and stockier. If the young mom were a man, people would call him husky. As it was, the young mom reminded Raina of a thick oak tree that could topple over a building or Raina's slender frame in a storm.

"Excuse me," Raina called out, waving her hand to get the young mom's attention. She didn't know what she wanted to say, but her gut told her to stall the woman. "You dropped something." She pointed at a crumpled receipt next to a potted plant behind the young mom.

The young mom tucked her head even lower. "That's not mine."

Raina hurried over until she stood in front of the stroller and blocked the young mom from leaving. "You didn't even look. It fell out of the basket underneath your stroller."

The young mom's hands tightened on the stroller.

She glanced over her shoulder. "Still not mine." She tried to sidestep with the stroller, but Raina moved with her.

"You shouldn't litter in paradise," Raina said. A bead of sweat rolled down the small of her back. If her gut was wrong, she might get arrested for harassing this poor woman. She glanced over the woman's shoulder to see Matthew looking at the trashcan outside the restroom building.

The young mom glanced up and spat, "Get out of my way."

Raina gasped. The face underneath the wide-brim hat looked just like the woman sitting next to her grandma in the minivan. "Leilani? How..."

The Leilani doppelgänger's eyes widened, but there was no moment of recognition. This person was a stranger. She hesitated for a fraction of a second and rammed the bassinet stroller into Raina's stomach. "I said get out of my way."

Raina staggered backward, clutching her midsection. "Help," she gasped into her smartwatch.

"What's going on?" Po Po said with alarm in the earpiece.

Over the Leilani doppelgänger's shoulder, Raina saw Matthew jerk up from the trashcan. His gaze swept the area and connected with hers for a brief moment. And then he sprinted toward Raina—running as if his life depended on it.

The Leilani doppelgänger shoved the stroller at

Raina one more time, tipped it forward on its front wheels, and pushed the whole stroller on top of her.

Raina stumbled back a step, trying to avoid pushing back at the stroller and hurting the baby inside. She tripped on her sandals and fell onto the ground, the stroller slamming down next to her. Was the baby okay? She didn't hear any crying.

The Leilani doppelgänger took off like a shotgun blast.

Matthew ran up to Raina, helping her off the ground. "Are you okay?"

Raina nodded and pointed after the Leilani doppelgänger. "She looks like Leilani's clone."

Matthew took off after the woman. His legs were a blur of activity.

With shaking hands, Raina got up and pulled the bassinet stroller upright. She yanked the blanket off and exhaled in relief. Inside, instead of a baby, was a stuffed monk seal.

The mom-and-baby disguise was brilliant. The Leilani doppelgänger must have tossed the diaper next to the trashcan on purpose so she could bend over to grab the ransom money and the diaper at the same time.

Raina held the smartwatch next to her mouth. "The pick-up person looks just like Leilani."

"Leilani is right next to me in the minivan," Po Po said in the earpiece.

"Do we have a clone or robot running around here?" Raina asked, trying to lighten the mood.

There was the sound of someone talking in the background, and then Leilani came on the line. "Not a clone or robot. That's my twin sister."

Now that Leilani confirmed it, Raina vaguely remembered there was a set of twin girls in the family.

"Isn't she the kidnapped victim?" Raina asked. What a colossal betrayal.

"Yes," Leilani said with anger in her voice. "This is another one of Ailani's tricks to get money out of the family."

Crash!

Raina spun around and saw Matthew sprawled on the ground in the food court. Several chairs lay on their sides. His face twisted in pain, his hands clutching his right foot. Raina's heart stopped for half a second before resuming its regular rhythm. She ran over to her husband, abandoning the stroller.

With Raina's help, Matthew got off the ground. When he tried to put weight on his right foot, he grimaced in pain. "I think something is broken."

3

SCAMMED

A quick trip to the emergency room confirmed that Matthew had indeed broken a tiny bone in his foot. If he had worn his sneakers instead of sandals, he might have saved himself several weeks in a cast. By the time the motley crew returned to the resort, everyone was hangry—that special blend of hunger and anger that could set someone off at the smallest thing.

Leilani dropped them off at the circular drive in front of the Aloha Village Resort and went to park the minivan. The twenty-acre family resort had one three-story main building. The first floor of the main lobby had all the typical amenities—a fitness room, a business center, a banquet room that could be converted to a conference room, a restaurant with a bar, a small convenience store, and a beauty center that offered haircuts, makeup, and spa services. While not quite run down, the resort was one of the most affordable properties on the island. The land was worth more money than all of the structures on it.

The pool lay between the main building and the patio dining area for the nightly luau and dinner show. A small grove of kukui trees, palm trees, and other tropical flora surrounded the patio dining area on three sides to screen off non-ticketed guests. Individual huts were scattered throughout the property between potted palms and other tropical flora. The honeymoon suite was one of the bigger huts, and Raina and her family gathered there to order room service for a late lunch.

As Raina watched her family stuff their faces, she had a feeling her suite would become the headquarters for their Hawaiian adventure. Po Po and Win had adjacent standard rooms in the main building, which were too small to fit everyone.

And yes, Raina assumed her honeymoon was officially over. It was probably over the moment her grandma's coconut bra fell off onstage. Other women might get peeved in her current situation, but Raina couldn't imagine telling her family that her suite was off-limits. Wherever she was, her home had always been defined by the family around her. And while her husband might grumble over losing their privacy, he was always good-natured about it.

Once they ate their fill and discussed the ransom drop-off—which resulted in more questions than answers—they left Matthew to watch TV. He was not a happy camper, but Raina knew he needed the quiet time to sleep off the heavy lunch and painkillers.

Once outside the suite, Win glanced around the beach and spotted the rental shack and the crowd of young people in front of it, waiting for their water gear such as snorkel equipment, canoes, and kayaks. He strolled off. "Catch up with you guys at dinner," he called out over his shoulder.

Raina rolled her eyes at her brother's back. "The beach and girls in bikinis."

"At least he knows his priorities," Po Po said.

The two of them shared a look and burst out laughing.

"Win is trying too hard to be a smooth operator," Raina said.

"When the right girl shows up, he'll knock it off," Po Po said.

The two of them strode down the meandering path toward the outdoor dining area set aside for the luau dinner show. The location was roped off, but it was easy enough for Raina and Po Po to duck under it.

Raina glanced around the empty food bar and picnic benches. The area had seemed larger in the evening under flickering tiki torches. As she stepped around a short palm tree with fan-shaped leaves, she saw an older woman with Leilani in an intense discussion on the stools of the closed tiki bar. "Is that Auntie May?" It had been years since Raina last saw the matriarch of the Hawaiian branch of the Wong family.

Po Po nodded. "Looks like trouble in paradise."

As they approached the bar, Auntie May shook her head in disbelief. "There has to be a mistake."

Auntie May was the Polynesian half of the Chinese-Polynesian family. She was stocky like her granddaughters and dressed in a muumuu with a matching orchid clipped to the side of her head. She was two years older than Po Po, but her hair was still salt and pepper. Her skin was weathered, and the crow's feet around her warm brown eyes were deep enough to need their own ladder.

Leilani gestured at Raina and Po Po. "We all saw Ailani. There's no mistake. Po Po can probably send you the mall's video feed."

Auntie May propped her elbows on the bar and rubbed her temples. "How can Ailani do this to us? I've been worried about her this entire time."

"After last year's scam, I thought we weren't giving her any more money," Leilani said with barely suppressed anger in her voice.

Raina raised an eyebrow at Po Po. This had happened before? The polite thing would be to give Auntie May and Leilani some privacy. But if they didn't care about airing their dirty laundry in front of Raina, why should she feel embarrassed for them? And it was interesting to learn that Ailani was the prodigal granddaughter while Leilani labored in the family business.

Who knew identical twins could be so different on the inside?

Po Po's bright eyes swiveled back and forth between Auntie May and Leilani. This supposed kidnapping represented everything Po Po loved about soap operas and murder mysteries. Her grandma wasn't someone who could spend hours lounging at the beach and sipping a cold drink. Her fingers twitched, almost as if she was forcing herself to keep from clapping in excitement.

"We can't report this to the police," Auntie May said. "We're family, and we have to stick together."

"So you want to flush ten thousand dollars down the toilet," Leilani said.

"That's not what I'm trying to say. We should get in touch with your sister and ask her to return the money."

"Like that will happen. With Ailani's gambling problem, the money will be gone by tomorrow."

Raina grimaced inwardly. Gambling addiction was the bane of most Chinese families. There was always a distant uncle, aunt, or cousin who got destroyed by it.

"Besides, we can't trust Tim Mars," Auntie May said. "If he finds Ailani with the cash, he'll keep it for himself. Or some of it might go missing."

"Is corruption such a big problem? Is Tim a local cop?" Raina asked. Her hometown police department might lose evidence once in a while due to incompetence, but she didn't think any of her husband's coworkers was actually corrupt. And did the corruption extend beyond the small village's local department to include the entire force on the island?

Auntie May and Leilani swiveled their eyes to stare at Raina. Oops. She probably should have kept her mouth shut.

"Yes, Tim is a cop," Leilani said. "My sister and I both dated him once."

Raina's eyes widened. They both dated the corrupt cop? "At the same time?"

"Separately. At different times," Leilani said tersely. "In my case, it didn't last more than a month. He thinks he's God's gift to women."

"How long did Ailani date him?" Po Po asked.

Auntie May sighed. "Too long."

"For a couple years they have been on and off. They might have broken up recently or they might be together." Leilani shrugged. "It's hard to keep track of it."

"I always suspected he introduced her to the illegal gambling on the island," Auntie May said. "Why else would she need cash like this?"

"It could be drugs," Po Po said.

Auntie May shook her head. "She doesn't have the look of a drug addict."

Leilani turned back to Auntie May. "You are such an enabler. Ailani has never helped around here, but she feels entitled to the family money. We are not doing so great that we can afford to burn money like this. Each year, the big resorts put more and more pressure on the little guys like us to sell up."

Raina wondered if there was a rivalry between the twins. If it extended to the men they dated, then it probably ran pretty deep. And if this was the case, then Leilani's words might be biased.

"We have enough. We can afford to help your sister out," Auntie May said.

"No, we do not," Leilani said, her eyes flashing with anger. "The compressor for the AC unit is on its last leg, and the walk-in freezer in the kitchen is always breaking down. We're lucky no one has gotten food poisoning yet from the luaus."

Raina cringed inwardly. Yikes! She couldn't wait to tell her husband this bit of news. Maybe after this, he might be willing to spend some money and take her out to dinner.

"And we can't expand our event-planning services without additional money," Leilani continued. "If we don't evolve, we will not survive the next ten years. The ransom money could have gone a long way reinvested back into the resort."

Auntie May sighed again. This was apparently a long-standing argument. "We have to make allowances for your sister. She witnessed your parents' death."

"Which was a long time ago," Leilani said. "It's not like I had an easy time with it either. I lost my parents too." Her voice wobbled, and she took a deep, shuddering breath. "But we all put on our big girl's panties and got on with life."

Auntie May patted Leilani's shoulders. "I know, hon, but you're the strong one."

Leilani shrugged off Auntie May's hand. "Ailani got more therapy than I did. She got more sympathy than I did. And there has never been any expectation for her to carry on. Every year, she gets thousands of dollars from us, and then we don't hear from her for months. I am just sick of this. So sick of this double standard. I am so sick of being the good girl. The responsible one."

"Then go," Auntie May whispered. Her voice was thick with emotion. "I don't need you to stay here to take care of me."

Leilani blanched as if her grandma had just slapped her. She got up on shaky legs from the barstool and stalked back to the main building.

Raina and Po Po shared a long look. Her grandma tipped her head in the direction of the building. Raina grimaced inwardly. Time to play Armchair Therapist. How in the world did she sign up for this? She got up and ran after her cousin.

Raina caught up to Leilani at the pool patio. "Leilani, wait!"

Her cousin paused mid-step. Several emotions flashed through her round face before she settled on being polite. "Rainy, do you need something?"

Raina shook her head. "I wanted to see if you need a friendly ear."

Leilani hesitated. She opened her mouth—

"I was also the good girl after my dad died," Raina said before her cousin had a chance to say no. "My older sister and mom fell apart, and I had to help my grandparents raise my baby brother." Her mouth twisted into a bitter smile. "I was still a child, but you know how it is. Teenagers always think they are more grown-up than they actually are."

Leilani took a deep breath and exhaled audibly. "I could use a drink. Want to join me?"

Raina glanced over her shoulder back in the direction of where they left the grandmas. "At the tiki bar?"

Leilani shook her head. "The restaurant has a bar. At this hour, it's practically empty."

"Lead the way," Raina said. She was a lightweight when it came to alcohol, but she was good at nursing one drink and listening to the other person's tale of woe. And from her experience, a drunk always had a woe-is-me story.

Raina was curious about the dynamics in the Hawaiian branch of the Wong family. Why was Ailani the black sheep? And how come the twins weren't close? Raina had always thought twins were best friends for life. She knew what folks said regarding curiosity, but she was family. It was okay for her to dig up these family secrets. And her grandma probably agreed with her.

4

A SUBSTITUTE

The Wayfarer was a family restaurant designed similarly to the big Chinese restaurants in San Francisco where panels with frosted glass could be moved around the restaurant to create banquet rooms for weddings and parties. The decor was mostly Hawaiian with a hint of a nautical theme.

The bar was at the front of the restaurant, to the left of the host station. A handful of high bar tables and chairs decorated with natural grass table skirts. The mirror behind the bar and the window walls created an illusion of a big and open space. A big flat-screen TV hung on the wall in the corner, showing a football game. A man sat in one corner, nursing his drink and scrolling through his phone.

Leilani slid into a seat at the bar table furthest from the TV. "What do you want?"

Raina slid onto the opposite stool. "Surprise me. Whatever the tourists usually get."

"You don't want what's on the menu," Leilani said. "There's a secret menu." She glanced over at the bar and held up two fingers in the air. "Hey, Big Mac."

The bartender nodded and set down the glass he was polishing. He grabbed two tall glasses from underneath the bar and set them in front of him.

Raina shifted her gaze back to her cousin. Was Leilani a secret alcoholic? Or did she only get this secret menu cocktail when she was at the restaurant bar? Raina was intrigued by this distant relative and the unfolding family drama. It was like being part of a reality show. "How does he know what drink to make?"

"Big Mac invented the Leilani for me. It's the only drink I get when I'm here," Leilani said, a blush coloring her cheeks.

Raina raised an eyebrow. Oooh la la. Was there romance in the air? She sneaked a glance at the bartender.

Big Mac was not all that big. He was tall, maybe six feet, two inches but so thin that he was a sneeze away from flapping in the wind. His watered-down blue eyes were cold and distant. His thick, blond, shoulder-length hair—his crowning glory—was pulled back into a ponytail. He wasn't an attractive man, but there was no accounting for other people's tastes. After all, Leilani appeared to feel like a lucky girl to have a drink named after her.

"I'm assuming that's a nickname," Raina said.

Leilani nodded. "He got that in high school because he could polish off three of those hamburgers in a sitting. It kind of stuck with him. His real name is Shawn Fisher."

Raina leaned forward, smelling dirt. "The two of you went to high school together?"

"He was my friend's boyfriend at the time." Leilani paused for a moment, deep in thought. "I can still see the two of them together," she muttered to herself.

"How long has he worked here?"

"Since high school. He started as a busboy at the restaurant."

"That's a long time. Doesn't he want to do something else?"

"For a while, we thought he would leave the island. But he injured his knee and got addicted to opioids, and then he lost his basketball scholarship." Leilani shrugged. "He disappeared off the radar for a few years. When he came back and asked grandma for a job, she couldn't say no. He grew up in the foster system, and we are the closest thing to family for him."

"Is he still addicted to painkillers?"

Leilani shook her head.

When the bartender brought over the drinks—a swirl of yellow, peach, a hint of light purple in the tall glasses with a small paper umbrella as a garnish—Leilani introduced Raina to Big Mac. They exchanged pleasantries, and the bartender went back to his work.

Leilani took a long gulp, finishing half of the cocktail. She closed her eyes and sighed; the tension appeared to leave her shoulders.

Raina took a small sip of the drink. The hint of lychee and green tea flavor hit her taste buds with a bang, and there was enough vodka in it to put an elephant to sleep. So Leilani might be a secret alcoholic after all. "I'm a good listener if you want to talk. I know what it's like to be the good girl in the family and feeling as if you're being punished for it."

And she did. For a short while, she was the temporary custodian for several million dollars after her grandfather's death. Her cousins were upset at Raina for supposedly inheriting this wealth while they got nothing. And when the secret finally came to light, Raina was more than happy to surrender the money to her uncle and let him deal with the distribution of it.

"I hate to ask, but why do you think Ailani went... off course?" Raina asked. "I'm assuming she wasn't always like this."

"It wasn't just our parents' death. Our best friend died in a car accident in high school, and I think Ailani always felt guilty about it." Leilani picked up her glass with shaking hands. She took a big gulp. "But done is done." She glanced down at her glass and finished off her drink. "Do you want another one?"

Raina shook her head.

Leilani raised her hand again to signal to Big Mac.

The bartender tipped his chin in acknowledgment.

"Give me a few minutes. I need to restock the glasses." He disappeared into the restaurant.

"Why does she feel responsible?" Raina asked.

Leilani stared into her empty glass. "She was the reason we didn't have dates that night. Her boyfriend had just dumped her."

"How will you get the money back?"

"I don't know. Ailani isn't going to give it to me because I asked for it. She used to do the bookkeeping at the resort, so she has plenty of experience to get a normal job. Then she'll have money like the rest of us."

"What did she do with the money gotten previously?"

Leilani shrugged. "Your guess is as good as mine."

Raina's cell phone chirped. She pulled it out of her purse and tapped on the screen. The message was from her husband.

"I'm getting hungry. Can you bring back snacks?"

Raina rolled her eyes. What a big baby. If he wanted snacks, he should call room service. She snorted. Right, like he would willingly pay for the additional cost? She glanced up from the screen and said, "I need to go. My hubby wants food. Do you need me to help you back to your apartment? Or someplace where you can rest a bit?"

Like the rest of the family members, Leilani lived in a studio apartment at the resort. Raina had no idea where the apartment complex was located, and she assumed it was nearby and hidden from the paying guests.

Leilani shook her head. "Don't worry about me. I can get back to my apartment with my eyes closed." There was a slight slur to her words, but she didn't sound incapacitated. And Big Mac would watch over her.

Raina glanced over at the bar. A blond man in the resort's uniform of a Hawaiian shirt and black trousers was at the bar. He wore aviator -framed glasses and had a big mole on the side of his chin. He set another Leilani drink on a tray. As long as someone was taking care of her cousin, it was probably okay to leave.

"I'll talk to you later," Raina said, hopping up from the barstool. "Knowing my husband, we'll be at the luau again tonight."

Leilani made the okay sign with her hand. Her cell phone rang, and she picked up the call. "Where are you, Ally?"

Raina paused mid-step. Was Ally short for Ailani? Was Leilani talking to her sister?

Leilani met Raina's eyes and made a shooing motion with her hand. "Private conversation, Rainy."

Raina gave her cousin an apologetic smile and strode away. If only there were a potted plant for her to hide behind. Eavesdropping was definitely harder in open spaces.

The bartender brought Leilani the second drink. He cleared off the dirty glasses and went back to the bar. Leilani picked up her drink, and with the cell phone next to her ear, strolled over to the bar.

Raina sighed inwardly. Time to deal with her big baby. Was this a sign of what to expect for the rest of her honeymoon? Fetching snacks for her husband? Babysitting her grandma and younger brother? At least the family drama was interesting.

WHEN RAINA STROLLED into the honeymoon suite a few minutes later, Matthew had his bad leg propped up on the coffee table, and he was watching the same football game on the bar TV.

The honeymoon suite was about the size of Raina's previous one-bedroom apartment. Barn-style doors closed off the king-sized bed and the two-person Jacuzzi tub from the living room area. On the first night that they had checked in, there was a giant heart made of rose petals on top of the comforters and a bottle of chilled champagne next to the bed.

The living room held a sofa set and a teak coffee table. The flat-screen TV was mounted on the wall. Scenic photographs of the island decorated the pale lemon walls. The microwave and coffeemaker sat on top of a small refrigerator in the corner of the room. The sliding glass doors opened out to a small patio where they could step right down to the beach.

Matthew's welcoming smile slipped when he saw

the bag of macadamia nuts. "I was hoping for buffalo wings." He opened the bag. "Or cheese fries."

"The nuts are healthier," Raina said, grabbing a handful. Her husband liked comfort food when he wasn't feeling good. Most of the time, this wasn't a problem, but with his broken foot, he would be in sloth mode.

As Matthew attacked the macadamia nuts, Raina filled him in on the family secrets she had uncovered from Auntie May and Leilani.

"I'm assuming we're done doing stuff for the family," Matthew said. He gestured at his leg. "It might be a little inconvenient, but I think we can still go jet skiing later."

"The whole point of a cast is to keep you from moving your foot," Raina said. And there was no way they were done with the family this early in their vacation. She just hoped the worst of it was over, and they could just sit back and watch the drama unfold in front of them.

Matthew waved dismissively. "I've had worse breaks than this and still fought off roadside bomb—"

Raina gasped. She knew he'd spent time in Afghanistan, but he never spoke of it. She had never seriously thought about what he had endured or witnessed.

Matthew flicked a glance at Raina's face. "Done is done, Rainy, and I am still here."

Raina reached across the sofa and gave him a bear

hug. It was more of a koala-size hug. Her grandparents were right: ignorance was bliss. By indirectly interfering with her relationship with Matthew in high school, they had saved her from years of worrying about his safety while he was in the Marines. She inhaled his sage and clean water scent. All that mattered was that he came back to her years later, whole and complete.

The beep of the electronic lock filled the air. The family had the lock code to the honeymoon suite. Raina untangled herself from Matthew and reached for the macadamia nuts. They both stared at the door expectantly.

Win strolled into the honeymoon suite and flopped down on the loveseat. He raised one hand dramatically to cover his forehead and said, "Sis, I'm in love."

Raina and Matthew shared a look and burst out laughing.

Win clutched his hands over his heart. "Ouch! You wound me."

Raina gave Win a deadpan stare. Her little brother had definitely inherited their grandmother's love for theatrics. "Oh, please. I just don't want to waste my time. You always break up with the girl by the time we're finally friends. Then it's awkward when I see them. It's like I don't know if I should greet them or ignore them."

Her younger brother had had girls chasing after him since he was fourteen years old. Luckily, he inherited their father's nerdy genes and was more interested in robotics and engineering. In high school, he had been oblivious to the attention. Even though he'd had dates for school functions and social events, he'd never dated seriously. The girl was usually gone after a few dates. Raina doubted this relationship of her brother's would last beyond the few days they were on the island.

Win gave Raina a hurt look. "It's different this time. There is something...magical about Jenny. I think she's the one."

Raina sighed inwardly. She would have no peace until Win finished talking about his new girl. "Okay. Why don't you invite her to join us for dinner tonight?"

Win shot Raina a look like she'd grown another head. "No, thanks. That's moving too fast. We just spent the afternoon together. It would scare Jenny off to meet the family this early in the game." He twirled a finger around the side of his head. "And our grandma is cray-cray. Sometimes, she even scares me."

Raina groaned. Game, huh? She didn't know her baby brother was such a player. Had he changed this much since the last time she had spent a few days with him? "Suit yourself. I don't want you whining later on about being neglected. This is me in my caring big sister mode."

The suite door banged open and Po Po sailed in with Auntie May in tow. Her grandma clapped her hands like she was marshaling the troops.

"Look alive, folks, look alive," Po Po said. "We can't find Leilani anywhere."

"Do you want us to join the search party?" Raina asked, confused. Leilani was probably still upset from her argument earlier with Auntie May. She might just be home with her cell phone turned off.

"I went to her apartment, but there wasn't anyone there," Auntie May said. "We need someone to replace her in the dinner show."

All eyes in the room swiveled to stare at Raina. The clock on the wall ticked for several loud seconds.

Raina's heart sank. She was never staying with family again. This obligation to help the host was getting ridiculous. "I don't know the Hawaiian dances."

"Win and I are dancing," Po Po said, gyrating her hips to make the point. One of them popped, and she ignored it. "We need you to be the emcee."

Raina's jaw dropped. What did she know about being the master of ceremony in a dinner show? Her gaze swiveled to her husband.

Matthew gave her a cheeky grin and two thumbs up.

Raina narrowed her eyes at him. He was enjoying this—the traitor. "I don't have the knowledge to introduce any of the dances or the folk tales."

Auntie May pulled out a stack of index cards from her muumuu and handed it to Raina. "It's all here. Just read through it a few times. You got this, Rainy. And if all else fails, make something up. The tourists are here for a good time, so they are more inclined to believe whatever you say."

"I already took one for the team," Matthew said, pointing at the cast on his foot. "It's your turn, Rainy. Do it for the kalua pork."

5

A LONG NIGHT

An hour later, Raina found herself backstage, dressed in a green leaf skirt, but thankfully with a tube top instead of a coconut bra. Around her head was a plastic Haku lei. The flower crown matched the plastic orchid lei around her neck. Fresh flower leis for the nightly dinner show would be a huge expense, and in the audience, no one would notice the difference. On Raina's wrists and ankles were shell bracelets and anklets. Each time she moved, something either rustled, jangled, or swished. There was no stealth mode in a Hawaiian costume.

An invisible strand of energy ran through everyone. Each person had a role—no matter how big or small—that could ruin the performance. There was a shared camaraderie that Raina had never experienced before. Was this why her great-grandma returned to the stage rather than stay as the third wife to her great-grandfather?

Auntie May thrust the microphone into Raina's hand. "Break a leg, Rainy. Have fun."

Raina grabbed the microphone and cell phone. It was show time. Knowing her luck, she wasn't taking chances with index cards. They would probably squirt out of her hands and scatter around her like confetti. No, thank you. She was going high-tech and had transcribed the information into the note app on her phone.

She plastered a beaming smile on her face and strode through the red velvet curtains. She squinted against the glare of the spotlight. Luckily, the audience was a sea of dark shapes where the occasional flickering tiki torches might illuminate a face well enough for Raina to make out the features. Her husband was at a front-row table, but her eyes were not adjusted enough to track him down. It was probably better this way.

Raina cleared her throat. "Ladies and gentlemen. We welcome you..."

She soon got into a groove where she introduced the dance, sashayed backstage to review her notes, and then came back to introduce the next segment of the show. It wasn't all that difficult to be the master of ceremony. Maybe she could turn this into a side gig. And watching the show from backstage gave her a new appreciation for all the performers. Even with torn costumes, sore muscles, one sprained ankle among the hula women, and a broken finger among the fire dancers, the show went on.

When Raina came back onstage for the third time, she could make out the cooks and performers by the imu, the underground oven on the beach. The ring of flickering tiki torches lit up the area. This was the most difficult part of the performance. She had to recite the folktale about the kalua pork and how this dish was a delicacy for the Hawaiian royalty. "But for tonight, you get to partake in this delicacy as our special guests," she said to the audience.

Raina walked off the stage and strolled across the dining patio to the beach, the spotlight following her every move. With the cooks opening up the imu behind her, Raina told the audience that the banana leaves-wrapped pig had been in the imu since last night, slow cooking on top of heated lava rocks for almost twenty-four hours. Her hair instantly reacted to the steam coming from the underground oven behind her. It recoiled and became a puffball around her head. The aromatic cooked-meat scent slowly wafted through the dining patio, and Raina's stomach growled. She wouldn't get to eat until everyone left. Maybe she could beg for a slice of meat or taro the next time she went backstage.

The spotlight shifted from Raina to the imu and

the cooks. Raina blinked rapidly, her eyes slowly adjusting to the dimness around her. With the audience focused on performers by the imu and the traditional dance thanking the gods for the food, Raina used this short reprieve to scan the audience. There! Her husband was at a front table to the left of the stage with his crutches propped up against a chair next to him. Her grandma peeked out from behind the closed stage curtains and ducked back in.

As a low murmur ran through the crowd, Raina frowned. In her stomach, a flutter of butterflies crashed into each other. She scanned the audience again, noting the shocked expressions. Two diners stood up and snapped photos of the imu opening ceremony. A woman cried out and fainted into her husband's arms.

The fine hair on Raina's neck stiffened. Something was wrong. Very wrong. Like a ventriloquist doll, she slowly turned around. The imu cover—a plank of plywood—lay on the sand next to the pit. The cooks had peeled back the layers of banana leaves to reveal the first layer of cooked taro and breadfruit. Bile rose up in Raina's throat. The second lumpy layer of steaming banana leaves covered a body curled up in a fetal position.

Raina was rooted to the spot, and if she panicked, the audience would follow her lead. She strode back onto the stage and gestured for the lighting crew to move the spotlight to her. She took a deep breath and announced the next dance. It was the men doing the fire dance, so hopefully it would shift the audience's attention from the imu. She trotted backstage and gestured for the men to start their act. She got off the stage area and ran to the trailer that served as a makeup and changing room.

Auntie May sat in a corner, whispering into her phone. When she caught sight of Raina, she waved for Raina to come over.

Po Po fell in step with Raina. "What happened out there? Did you forget your lines? I thought the fire dance was later in the program."

Auntie May held up her phone and looked at Raina expectantly. "The cook is babbling about a body in the imu."

This was not the first time Raina had encountered a body, but it didn't make the situation any easier. She took a deep breath and let it out. "There's a body underneath the banana leaves. I had to cut the ceremonial dance short. The audience probably saw it, too."

Auntie May gasped. Her phone fell out of her hands and landed with a crack on the floor. "Are you sure it wasn't the pig?"

"A pig can't get into the fetal position," Raina said.

Auntie May shook her head. "It's probably the lighting. It created the illusion of a body. Once we remove the banana leaves, we'll see a pig."

"That is the first worst thing we can do," Raina said. "Not only would it horrify the audience, but we will contaminate the crime scene."

"Crime scene?" Auntie May echoed. Her face turned ashen. "No."

"A person doesn't fall into an imu accidentally," Raina whispered. She gagged at the memory of the cooked meat scent and covered her mouth with a hand. She swallowed several times.

"What happened to the pig?" Po Po wondered out loud. Her grandma didn't appear fazed by the situation. This wasn't her first rodeo with a dead body. "That's like twenty pounds of meat."

"Who cares about the pig," Raina said. "We need to call the police and keep the crowd entertained until they get here." She snapped her mouth shut, disliking the rising hysteria in her voice. She had to keep it together because she was the ringleader of this circus. She took a deep breath and consciously made an effort to speak normally. "We can't let anyone leave the scene. The police will want to interview everyone."

"Who...who is in the imu?" Auntie May asked, her voice trembling.

Raina shrugged. "I don't know. I redirected the audience's attention to the stage. And the cooks stopped removing the banana leaves once they saw the body."

Auntie May nodded. "Right. Good idea."

"Should we cover up the imu again?" Po Po asked.

"I think it's okay to put the plywood cover back on. We don't want the audience to look at it the entire time during dinner," Raina said. "We can have Matthew guard the crime scene."

"Dinner?" Auntie May asked. "We're still serving dinner?"

"We have to keep the crowd from leaving before the police get here," Raina said.

"You can't make people unsee what they saw," Po Po said. "But food and drinks might make a difference. Everyone is probably hungry. And if we get them drunk, they can't dash off. Or it'll slow them down enough that we can tackle them."

Auntie May swayed slightly in her chair. ""Okay."

Po Po patted Auntie May's shoulder. "Deep breaths, May. Go talk to the staff and start the dinner service. Rainy can manage the crowd. And I'll get Matthew. He can call the police and take a look at the crime scene. Take care of business first. You can fall apart later."

For the next fifteen minutes, Raina forced herself to remain calm and cheerful. Even though her voice was a few decibels higher than usual, she didn't think the audience noticed. The jangle of the seashell jewelry on her wrists and ankles grated on her nerves, but her smile remained in place. Auntie May was counting on Raina to control the crowd, and she would not fail her family. The low murmur continued to get louder through the next two dances.

A man in a Hawaiian shirt and black cargo shorts waved to get Raina's attention. He pointed at the buffet bar and gave her a thumbs up.

Raina said to the audience, "A resort staff will come by your table to lead you to the food bar."

A man stood up and pointed at the imu. "You can't expect us to eat after seeing that."

All the eyes in the audience followed the man's finger like it was a laser beam. Luckily, Matthew had already extinguished the tiki torches around the underground oven. Raina could only see shadows beyond the lit dining patio.

A bead of sweat rolled down the small of Raina's back. She remembered her grandma's words backstage about food or drinks. "If you don't want to eat, you can have a drink. It's on the house. One of the resort staff will take your drink order."

Auntie May would have to take a loss on tonight's dinner show, but it was better to have no profit than the alternative. If the resort staff did their best to salvage the situation, maybe the police wouldn't shut down the show during their investigation. The outdoor dining patio offered too many exit routes. If the audience all got up to leave, the staff would be outnumbered. And the killer could be among the audience.

Raina shivered at a warm breeze. A person didn't fall into an underground oven pit and cover themselves up with several layers of banana leaves and vegetables by accident. She scanned the audience, but she couldn't see well enough to make out faces. No one jumped out as a suspect. If only the bad guy sat at a table, smirking and twirling a mustache.

Her shoulders grew tighter. Who was under the banana leaves? If it was a crime of passion, it would make more sense for the killer to ditch the body in some place more inconspicuous like one of the many overgrown ravines in the area. The nightly dinner show guaranteed that the body would be discovered within hours. Which meant the killer wanted the body discovered. Was this person punishing the victim or someone close to the victim? Was the killer counting on the staff to uncover the body publicly? Raina had no doubt this was some kind of revenge killing...and premeditated.

A couple got up and disappeared into the night. Raina hoped Matthew had posted someone to keep watch around the perimeter of the dining patio. The murmuring in the audience grew louder. Another couple got up to leave. As they were about to slip into the night, a man in plainclothes and several police officers blocked the couple's exit. They were directed back to their seats.

Raina exhaled in relief. The police got here just in time. A few more seconds, and she would have lost control of the audience.

The plainclothes police officer got up on stage, and Raina handed him the microphone gratefully.

"I am Detective Sergeant Tim Mars," the plainclothes cop said. "We need to get your contact information and statements." Two of the uniform officers went over to chat with Matthew by the underground oven.

With shaking legs, Raina slipped backstage and sank down on the ground. The tension slipped away from her shoulders. Her job was done for the night. She just had to sit tight until the police interviewed her.

6

WINGED PIGS

The police took statements from the audience first. There were close to two hundred guests and only five officers. This was probably the town's entire police department. Surprisingly, they even enlisted Matthew's help to speed up the process. As Raina watched her husband interview the audience, she felt a mixture of pride and envy.

As a homicide detective, former Marine, and contractor who took on top-secret assignments from the federal government, Matthew radiated credibility and quiet competence. Raina wished she had some of his *je ne sais quoi*—that "it" factor that made her husband so attractive. She often felt like a character in an *I Love Lucy* episode, especially with her grandma around.

After the last of the audience left an hour later, the police rounded up the staff in the dining patio. As the police began to interview the staff, Po Po strolled up to the food bar and began filling a plate.

Raina's stomach growled. Even though the food had been sitting out for a while, it was probably safe enough to eat. She glanced around. No one paid any attention to the food bar. She got up and casually joined her grandma.

"I can't believe the police got through the audience so quickly," Po Po said, setting her heaping plate on a dining table.

Raina set her plate down and pulled out the chair next to her grandma. "They probably just took down contact information and will follow up tomorrow." She bit into a cold chicken thigh and sighed. The meat was still succulent, though it was a bit dry. The rosemary and thyme seasoning was perfect.

With food in her mouth, Po Po said, "Matthew looks hangry. Maybe we should bring him a plate of food."

Raina glanced over her shoulder.

Someone had relit the tiki torches and moved the spotlight back to the underground oven area. Matthew stood in front of the imu, his injured foot resting on a corner of the plywood cover as if he was blocking access to the body. He faced off with two uniformed officers who were returning scowl for scowl. Instead of leaning on his crutch, he used the medical device like a pointer. Win strolled over and flanked Matthew. Even with just a grass skirt on, her younger brother radiated the same aura of strength as his brother-in-law. The two of them created a formidable barrier.

"He's not cranky from hunger," Raina said. "He's upset because the officers are disturbing the crime scene. Look at all the footprints on the sand. Where is the coroner?"

Po Po leaned forward eagerly. "Do you think Matthew needs backup? I always wanted to be his backup."

Raina bit into the cold chicken thigh again and chewed quickly. If things went south, she wanted to face it with a full stomach. "We should stay out of the way."

Detective Mars joined the men at the underground oven. Voices were raised, but Raina couldn't make out what they were discussing. Eventually, Matthew stalked off, which wasn't easy to do on crutches. Win followed his brother-in-law, and the two men joined Raina and Po Po at the table.

With the bottomless energy of a puppy, Win glanced at the plates of food, spun on his heels, and trotted to the food bar. Within minutes, several resort staff joined him. Soon, everyone had heaping plates and settled down at one of the dining tables. They watched as the police uncovered the underground oven.

Raina returned her attention to the food on her plate. She didn't want to see any of the gory details.

A few minutes later, someone tapped on Raina's shoulder. "Ma'am, I need to take your statement."

Raina glanced up into Detective Sergeant Tim Mars's piercing hazel eyes. She nodded and stood up. "Lead the way, Detective."

Detective Mars was probably in his mid-forties. He had long, skinny limbs that looked as if someone had forgotten to feed him. Maybe he should grab a plate of food from the buffet bar like everyone else. Nestled underneath his dirty, blonde hair were big, hazel eyes and a weathered babyface. His perfunctory smile was wide, but it lacked warmth.

He asked Raina for her name and contact information.

"Raina Sun Louie," Raina said.

Detective Mars jerked a thumb toward Matthew's direction. "Are you related to Matthew Louie?"

Raina groaned inwardly. She didn't like the disapproving undertone to the question. Where was his professionalism? "He's my husband."

Detective Mars's fake smile slipped. "Tell me what happened tonight?"

Raina told him what she saw and how she distracted the audience with food and drinks.

"Do you have any idea who might be in the underground oven?" Detective Mars asked, his pen poised over his notebook.

Raina gaped at him. Was he kidding? Or did he

think she was the killer? "I didn't peek under the banana leaves, so I don't know."

"It's always worth asking the question," Detective Mars said, closing his notebook. "Sometimes the answers come from the most unexpected places."

Raina didn't know how to respond. The detective had already contaminated the crime scene, and now he expected the witness to figure out the case like it was a *Clue* board game?

"If I remember something more, do you have a phone number I can call?" Raina asked, smiling. After the face-off next to the underground oven, she doubted that her husband could get information through the official channel.

Detective Mars scribbled a number on the back of a business card and handed it to her. "Here's my cell phone number. You can call any time." He winked.

Raina recoiled inwardly, and her smile stiffened. Was he leering at her? She pocketed the card. "Great."

THE NEXT MORNING, the family gathered at the Wayfarer restaurant for brunch. Even normally energetic Win ordered coffee this morning. At this hour, the restaurant was busy enough that no one paid any attention to their table.

After they placed their orders, Auntie May came by and sank into a chair. She looked like something the cat threw up. The wrinkles deepened even more, and dark circles ringed her eyes. She probably didn't sleep a wink last night after the coroner left with the body.

"Mei Mei, after we're done here, can you come with me to the police station?" Auntie May said, addressing Po Po as if she were a younger sister. It wasn't unusual in Chinese families for cousins to address each other like they were actually siblings.

"Not a problem. I got your back," Po Po said, pouring more gravy over her sausage and rice.

Raina didn't want to spoil her grandma's fun, but she might end up with a stomach ache from all that gravy. When her grandma set down the gravy boat, Raina discreetly moved it to the opposite end of the table. "Why do you need to go down to the police station?"

"They want me to help identify the body," Auntie May said. "I was hoping to see Leilani this morning, but I still haven't been able to reach her. She would have a better idea if there was anyone missing at the resort."

Po Po patted Auntie May's hand. "She can't stay mad at you forever." Her grandma was probably referring to the argument over Ailani and the ransom money at the tiki bar.

"The police didn't even get the contact information from everyone in the audience last night," Matthew said, shaking his head. "They contaminated the crime scene before the forensic team got there. Don't hold your breath. These people don't know what they are doing."

"Or care," Win added. "They are a bunch of idiots."

Matthew rolled his eyes at Raina, barely containing his amusement.

Raina snorted. One summer interning with their cousin, Lucy Fong, at her private investigation firm, and her baby brother became a crime-solving expert.

"I suggested they call the FBI in for help," Matthew continued. "But Detective Mars was offended."

Raina considered what her husband said. "Then we should help him out. Point him in the right direction. Or make it so the people in charge can't cover things up."

"This sounds mercenary, but we need to resume the dinner shows ASAP," Auntie May said. "I'm sorry someone is dead, but the alcohol tab alone pays for all the performers. And if I don't pay the performers, I might lose them. And once we resume the luaus again, it will be difficult to find skilled dancers.

Po Po nodded in understanding. "You have to keep paying them so that they don't jump ship, but you can't afford to pay them without money coming in."

"Exactly," Auntie May said. "We already canceled the show tonight, but I'm hoping we can have a show tomorrow. Fridays and Saturdays are our most profitable nights."

Raina knew Auntie May couldn't afford a prolonged shutdown of the dinner show. Her great-aunt had given Ailani ten thousand dollars in the kidnapping scam. And to top it off, hurricane season had started a few weeks ago, which meant tourism would drop off even more.

The server and her helper returned with plates of food and a cup of coffee for Auntie May. For the next few minutes, there were only the sounds of chewing and forks scraping the plates. It was the first time Raina had Portuguese sausage, eggs, and rice for breakfast.

Win sighed and sat back in his chair, rubbing his full stomach. "That hit the spot." He had even managed to scrape the runny egg yolk off his plate. "What's the game plan? Are we investigating or not?"

"Not," Raina said.

"Yes," Matthew said at the same time.

Raina gaped at her husband. "We're on our honeymoon, and we should be doing lovey-dovey stuff. Not chasing down suspects."

Win covered his ears. "Gross. It's like listening to your parents talk about their sex life."

"We are not that old," Raina said.

Po Po smacked Win on the arm. "Seriously, kiddo? You want to hear about my sex life instead?"

Matthew burst out laughing, and Raina choked on her coffee. Her brother deserved that comment.

Win flushed and lowered his hands. "Let's get back to the murder."

"Rainy, you can do lovey-dovey stuff when you get home," Po Po said. "We have to help Auntie May."

Matthew crossed his arms. "When you have the Three Stooges running the show, it's my professional duty to help."

Raina glanced up at the ceiling. There were no pigs in the air. "Who are you? And where is my husband?"

"I can't believe they called me an interfering bureaucrat," Matthew said. "After all the help I gave them. These people will not run a proper investigation."

Raina gave her husband a sideways glance. So that was it. He was upset because they thought he was a paper pusher. She snickered inwardly. Welcome to her world. Everyone always assumed her boyish petite figure also meant she came up short on the intelligence department as well.

Win pointed at the crutches resting next to Matthew's chair. "No offense, but how are you going to run this investigation?"

Matthew tapped the side of his head. "I can be the brains behind the operation. You guys are my boots in the field. I will man HQ."

"And where is the headquarters?" Po Po asked, her eyes glittering.

"The honeymoon suite," Matthew said matter-of-factly. "Where else would I hang out with my bum leg?"

Raina held up her hands and made the universal

time-out sign. "Whoa. Hold on for a minute. You're not suggesting that we investigate this murder outside of official channels, are you?"

Unlike Raina, who liked to throw the entire bowl of spaghetti on the wall during an investigation, Matthew was methodical, dotting every *I* and crossing every *T*. Granted, he needed the paperwork trail because his work had to stand up in court. The thought of investigating a murder with her husband gave her chills. Their marriage might not survive this.

Matthew nodded. "I know. I still can't believe the words coming out of my mouth either. Better take me up on it before I change my mind."

"Done," Po Po said. "No backsies after this. All of you are filling in for my Posse Club members. I don't have anyone else to boss around here." She tapped her chin. "I need to think up code names for us."

Win glanced at Raina and smirked. "So, who is in charge here?"

Raina narrowed her eyes at her brother. The rascal was an instigator. He was spending too much time with their grandma.

Win's gaze drifted to a spot over Raina's shoulder. His eyes widened, and he jerked up, scraping his chair on the wood floor.

7

THE GIRLFRIEND INTERVIEW

Raina turned around. A young brunette in her late twenties approached the table and waved at Win with a shy smile.

Po Po swiveled to stare at a flushing Win. Even the spot above his collar was a deep red.

Win grinned like he'd just won the lottery. Raina had never seen her brother's eyes sparkle like this when looking at a girl. He might actually be serious about this one.

Po Po mouthed to Raina, "A cougar. I like it."

Matthew choked on his coffee, coughing up brown splatters onto his napkin.

Raina bit the inside of her cheek to keep from laughing out loud. Her stoic husband appeared to be off-balance since the fake ransom drop-off—both emotionally and physically. She wasn't used to seeing this side of him. But, on the other hand, it was nice having someone else committing the social faux pas.

"This is Jenny Harris," Win said. "We met at the rental shack yesterday. We spent the afternoon kayaking." He introduced his family to his "friend."

"Do you want to join us for brunch, hon?" Po Po asked the young woman.

Jenny glanced at Win, who stood up to pull out the chair next to him. She was almost the same height as her brother in her flip-flop sandals. "Oookay." She sat down, equally as red as Win.

Raina smiled to herself. Her brother's love interest was just too cute for words.

Jenny Harris was attractive in the girl-next-door kind of way with her long, glossy brown hair and bright-blue eyes, the same shade of blue as her Hawaiian print maxi dress. When she smiled, her teeth looked unnaturally even and white against her tan. Her heart-shaped face was open and guileless like she wanted to please the family.

The server came over, refilled everyone's coffee mug, and took Jenny's order.

"Jenny, where are you from?" Po Po asked, leaning forward in her chair. And so, the Twenty-one Questions game began.

The questions usually boiled down to family, education, and profession. It wasn't so much that Po Po was a snob, but she didn't want a girlfriend who might resent a large, close-knit family. And to add to the pressure, Raina's uncles, aunts, and cousins all held a long list of alphabets after their names and were successful in their occupations.

However, the Sun branch of the family was the exception. Their mother was the youngest of Po Po's children and a socialite. Their older sister was a stay-at-home mom. Even Raina with her degrees felt like a screwup at times because she didn't follow the traditional path of moving up in a profession. With her part-time jobs, Raina didn't have much to brag about other than that her bills got paid on time. But, at least her life was never dull.

Win shot Raina a pleading look as if asking her to intervene.

Raina sat back in her chair and smirked at her brother. According to their grandma, embarrassment was good for the soul and kept a person humble.

As it turned out, Jenny Harris used to be a local, but her family moved to the Big Island a few years ago after her older sister's death in a car accident.

"This sounds kind of silly, but the anniversary of my sister's death is coming up," Jenny said. Her eyes were fixed on a spot on the table in front of her. "I thought it might be nice to visit her. My dad thought I was silly, but my mom supported the idea. I guess that's why they are divorced."

Po Po nodded. "I don't think it's silly at all. It's normal in Chinese culture to visit the dead. Once a year, we even have a party at the cemetery to honor our ancestors."

Her grandma was referring to the Ching Ming Festival, where Chinese families swept the ancestral burial ground to get rid of cobwebs and bugs. In the old village, they didn't have groundskeepers, so it was up to the family to keep things tidy. And it eventually became an annual tradition where the families brought food, wine, joss paper, and incense to make offerings to their ancestors and ask for their blessing. These days it was a family party at the graveyard.

"What do you do for a living?" Po Po asked. "You look a little bit mature for our Win."

Raina pressed her lips together and averted her gaze. Her younger brother looked as if he wanted to die on the spot. She could sense her husband's amusement. If they made eye contact, the two of them would burst out laughing.

"I'm an assistant cinematographer," Jenny said. "I am in between projects, so it was the perfect time to get away."

Before Po Po could drill down to the Harris family dynamics, Auntie May tapped her arm. "Bonnie, we still need to go down to the police station."

Several expressions crossed Po Po's face as if she was torn between staying and leaving. She sneaked a glance at Auntie May's face and made up her mind. "I'm ready to rock 'n' roll." She nodded at Jenny. "Don't be a stranger, honey. We always have room for one more at our dinner table."

Win sagged into his chair. His new girlfriend had passed the test.

Po Po, Auntie May, and Win headed toward the staff parking lot. Her younger brother was the unofficial chauffeur for the retirees. Jenny opted to wait for Win's return at the beach.

In some ways, Raina was glad Jenny would distract her younger brother from the murder investigation. The last time he had helped, he almost got into trouble with the murderer. And she didn't want it to happen again this time. As the baby of the family and only son, their mother would kill Raina if anything happened to her precious Little Emperor.

"I'm going to find Leilani," Raina said. "As the operations manager, she needs to know about what happened last night. Even if she is hung over, she has to take care of business. It's too much for Auntie May to take on at her age."

"Do you want me to come with you?" Matthew asked.

Raina flicked a glance at his crutches. "Sorry, but you'll just slow me down." She gave him a cheeky grin. "For the first time, you can't keep up with me, old man."

"Yeah, yeah. Kick me while I'm down," Matthew said, smiling back at her. "I'll go man HQ and make some phone calls."

"Who are you calling?"

"It's need-to-know, Rainy. And you don't need to know."

Raina rolled her eyes. If it made him feel better to make phone calls to his top-secret connections, she didn't care. He was probably still upset at himself for tripping on a chair and breaking his foot. It was a booby trap set up by an amateur, and as a professional, it probably stung his pride a bit. "Uh-huh." She patted his cheek gently. "Talk to you later, Elly."

Matthew's first name was Elliot, but he liked to go by his middle name. Whenever they were alone, she liked to tease him with her childhood nickname for him.

While the staff finished the lunch service in the dining area, the bar in the front of the restaurant was starting to get busy. People straggled in, ordering exotic cocktails in long thin plastic cups and heading back to the beach. Big Mac was the only one mixing drinks at the bar. Maybe the other bartender only came in to help with the evening crowd.

Raina slid onto a seat at the bar. "Hi, Big Mac. I don't know if you remember me, I'm Raina Sun Louie, Leilani's second cousin. I was here with her yesterday afternoon."

Big Mac's watered-down blue eyes flicked to Raina's hair, and he tipped his chin. "I can't understand how a beautiful woman like Leilani could have a cousin with such awful hair. But yeah, I remember you."

Raina gave him a deadpan stare. Just because he had nice hair, didn't mean he could go around criticizing other people's hair. Geez. She could make a comment about his twig-like arms, but she was taking the high road. "Anyways," she said, shaking off his comment, "I am looking for Leilani. No one has seen her since yesterday afternoon. Have you seen her? Do you know where I can find her?"

Big Mac continued to mix drinks. "I don't get paid enough to be her keeper." His tone was just a hair short of being hostile. Weren't bartenders supposed to be friendly people?

"When I left yesterday, she was on her second drink," Raina said. "Do you know how long she stayed here? And did she meet or talk to anyone? That was the last time anyone saw her. The family is trying to figure out if she is somewhere sleeping off a hangover or if something bad happened to her."

"If May wants to know, she can call me," Big Mac said.

Even if Raina got Auntie May on the phone, Big Mac wouldn't spill any secrets. She had questioned people enough times to know he would only supply one- or two-word answers.

"Can I get a virgin Leilani?" Raina said. The words sounded weird coming out of her mouth. "I'm a lightweight when it comes to alcohol."

Big Mac grunted and began making the cocktail

drink. In a few minutes, he slid the drink across the bar to Raina.

"Why did you name a drink after Leilani?" Raina asked, sipping the cold beverage. The lychee and green tea flavors tasted even better without the alcohol. The only thing missing would be a scoop of vanilla ice cream.

"Why not?" Big Mac said. He picked up a towel and began wiping down the bar.

"Did you name a drink after Ailani?"

"No."

"Can you name a drink after me?" Raina asked. She was only making conversation, hoping to ease into her later questions."

"No."

Raina raised an eyebrow. "So just Leilani, huh? Do you have a crush on her or something?"

Big Mac paused mid-swipe, considering Raina. "Aren't you married? Why are you flirting with other men?"

Raina choked on her drink. If asking a few nosey questions was the equivalent of flirting to this guy, he obviously didn't spend much time around women. But if she pointed this out, he might clam up even more. Now how could she say this without hurting his feelings?

"I'm happily married," Raina said. "It's always good to talk to people because you never know what oppor-tunities are available." She gave him a warm smile.

"Besides, Leilani said you're easy to talk to. So I figure you're like my hairdresser, and I can just chat with you."

"I am not your hairdresser. And I am not one of your girlfriends. Take your chatting elsewhere." Big Mac turned, picked up a bottle on the wall shelf, and wiped underneath it. He made slow, deliberate progress through all the bottles on the wall.

Raina sat back a little bit miffed. Why was he this unfriendly? Was it because she didn't tip well enough for the free drinks? As a VIP member at the resort, Raina got the drinks free, so she had no idea how much they cost. Wasn't two dollars a decent tip? She took a deep breath and tried again. "Did you hear about what happened last night at the luau?"

Big Mac paused his wiping for half a heartbeat. If Raina wasn't looking for it, she might have missed it. He turned around and threw the towel on the bar and crossed his arms. "What happened?"

His posture and tone were still unfriendly, but Raina could tell he wanted information. The piped-in beach music filled the space between them.

Raina took a long sip of her cocktail, stretching out the moment. "It's kind of strange you haven't heard the news."

"I just got here half an hour ago. My shift starts later than everyone else because the bar stays open later. I haven't even gotten a chance to talk to anyone yet."

"Where is Leilani's apartment? I know the staff housing is somewhere on the resort property, but I don't know how to get there."

Big Mac pressed his lips into a thin line, reached underneath the bar, and pulled out a paper map. He pointed to an area in front of the circular driveway of the resort. "If you go through the patch of forest, you'll get to the staff apartment complex. It's a fifteen minute walk straight through. Just stay on the path. Leilani is in 2B."

Raina blinked. He must really want to know what happened last night. He was almost too helpful. "How long have you worked at the resort?"

"Why is this relevant?"

"Just wondering how invested you are in the resort's success."

"I started bussing the tables at the restaurant in high school and then did grounds maintenance for a while," Big Mac said. "May has treated me well through all these years."

"Did you want to be a bartender or did you fall into it by accident?"

"There aren't that many job options on the island," Big Mac said. "Is this enough friendly banter for you? Can you tell me what is going on?"

"Why do you think Ailani is the black sheep of the family?"

Big Mac gave her a cold stare. "You've asked for

Leilani's home location, and I gave it to you. I think it's your turn to fulfill our bargain."

Raina told him about the body in the underground oven.

Big Mac's eyes widened. "Who...who is the victim?"

Raina was surprised at how quickly he came to the conclusion there was foul play. Was there something else going on at the resort that led to this murder? She shook her head. "I don't know. Did you notice anything suspicious yesterday?"

"No, I didn't see anyone dragging a dead body around the resort, if that's what you're asking."

"Who worked with you yesterday?" Raina asked. "Maybe the other bartender might have seen something." And maybe the other bartender might be chattier.

"I was the only one working."

Raina frowned, trying to recall the other bartender's features. "He's tall, blond, and wears glasses." She pointed to the side of her chin. "He has a black mole here."

Big Mac shrugged. "I still don't know what you're talking about."

"Who made Leilani's second drink?"

Big Mac narrowed his eyes. "What are you? Some kind of amateur detective?"

"Nooo," Raina said slowly. "Auntie May wants things to return to normal as soon as possible. I'm just helping her ask some questions. To see if the staff noticed anything."

Raina's curiosity had gotten her into trouble before, but it also added memorable moments of excitement. It helped her understand the people around her. It was her weakness and also her strength.

Big Mac picked up his towel and resumed wiping the bar again. "You know what they say about curiosity. You don't want to be a dead cat."

Raina picked up her drink, slipped five dollars onto the bar, and left. She held herself ramrod straight, afraid that she might shiver from the chill in his voice. What was up with this guy? Did he behave like this with everyone, or did she win a special lottery and get on his bad side? Why would Auntie May keep him around?

A few minutes later, when Raina opened the door to the honeymoon suite, she could tell from the silence that Matthew wasn't in the room. She used the restroom and left. With nothing else better to do, she might as well knock on Leilani's door. This cat was getting satisfaction one way or the other.

8

CLOSE TO HOME

As Raina strolled back to the lobby area again, she texted her plan to Matthew. With the spotty cell phone coverage on the island, she didn't expect him to answer. Sometimes messages showed up hours later, long after the recipient needed the information. They might need to get walkie-talkies, which would make her grandma happy.

Once through the lobby and outside, facing the circular driveway, Raina felt a pang of unease. The forest in front of her appeared thick and impenetrable, more like a rainforest than the familiar redwoods, oaks, Douglas firs, and spruces in the woods back home. She only recognized the kukui trees because of their distinctive light-green foliage and nuts. Being a city person, all the greenery made her skin itch.

A resort staff wearing a bold Hawaiian shirt and black trousers stepped out of a narrow opening in the forest. He crossed the circular driveway and nodded at her.

Raina turned around, watching the resort staff stroll into the main building. The uniform wasn't exactly unique. Almost anyone could cobble together the outfit from the lobby convenience store. If the killer dressed like the rest of the staff, this person could move around the resort unnoticed, including lugging a disguised body. And if questioned by a staff, this person could pretend to be a new employee.

She pulled out her cell phone and tapped in a reminder to look at the video feed. Hopefully, the security system wasn't on its last leg like the air compressor.

Raina trotted to the narrow opening, plunging into another world. Blinking, her eyes adjusted to the sudden dimness. Every buzz, gurgle, and squawk sounded louder than when she was outside the forest, as if someone had turned up the volume on the radio. Even the air itself was heavy with moisture and made her skin sticky. Overhead, patches of the blue sky filtered in between the branches. She turned around and could see the opening that she came through, but the foliage created a thick wall, blocking the resort from view.

Logically, Raina knew the forest was only a few acres, but what if she got lost in here and never came out? Unlike a city neighborhood block, the dense forest didn't have signs to guide her out. She took a deep breath. Big Mac had said it was a short walk, and

Raina didn't plan to deviate from the path in front of her. She would be okay. Besides, she had gone on plenty of hikes out in nature. This was no different.

The short walk ended up taking twenty-five minutes. Halfway through, there was a fork on the path, and she went down the branch that led to a ravine and a flock of wild chickens. She had to retrace her steps. By the time the path opened to a clearing and a dreary three-story apartment building, Raina was not in the best of moods. Her hair was limp and matted against her head. She was thirsty, sticky with sweat, and a little jumpy.

The concrete box with metal railings didn't have an ounce of charm, and forget about a beachfront view for the family and staff members who lived on site. That amenity was reserved for the paying guests outside the forest. Laundry hung out on a couple of the balconies. Maybe the dryer was broken. Wouldn't the moisture in the air cause the clothes to get moldy?

Raina strolled to the front of the building. A few older-model vehicles were in the small, gravel parking lot. The gravel road that led out of the forest was probably connected to the main road.

Raina trudged upstairs on the staircase to the second floor, flapping the neck of her T-shirt and hoping for a breeze. *Please let there be air conditioning in the apartment.*

Raina knocked on 2B's door.

Silence.

She knocked again.

Nothing.

Maybe she should have called first before trekking over here to find an empty apartment. Pressing one ear against the door, Raina pulled out her cell phone and dialed Leilani's number. She heard shuffling inside the apartment but no ring tone. Maybe her cousin's cell phone was in silent mode.

The door opened, and Raina crashed onto the floor, landing on her hip. Pain ran down her leg, and Raina drew in a sharp breath. She glanced over to see Leilani looking down at her with a shocked expression. Her cousin was in a bathrobe and slippers. Her hair was pulled back into a messy bun.

"Thanks a lot, Coz," Raina said. She didn't bother hiding the annoyance in her voice. She thrust out her hand.

Leilani stared at Raina's hand like it was an alien object.

Raina wiggled her fingers. "Aren't you going to help me up?"

Leilani grabbed Raina's hand and hauled her off the ground.

Raina brushed the seat of her pants and rubbed her sore hip. Her second cousin was one strong woman. "Where have you been? Auntie May has been worried about you. Was it the second drink? Did you have to sleep it off?"

"What are you doing here?" Leilani asked, crossing her arms in front of her chest.

Raina blinked at her cousin's unfriendly body language. Geez, Leilani sounded just like Big Mac. Maybe the two of them were a secret couple, after all. Was she embarrassed for drinking so much yesterday?

"What do you think?" Raina said. "I'm looking for you. I even had to fill in for you as the master of ceremony at the dinner show last night. And boy, did you miss a good show."

Leilani still blocked the entrance to her apartment. "Sorry, but it's not a good time right now." She rubbed her temples, wincing. "Why don't we talk later, uh...Cousin?"

Raina placed her hands on her hips. Apparently, a hungover Leilani wasn't a nice person. "I am sweaty and cranky. I got lost coming through that forest back there." She flapped a hand in the general direction of the forest. She was channeling her inner Po Po. Her grandma wouldn't take no for an answer. "I want a nice cold drink. And I am not leaving until I get it."

Leilani narrowed her eyes. Raina returned the stare. As the visiting family member, if Raina held her ground, Leilani would eventually give in.

"Fine," Leilani said, throwing her hands up in the air. She headed toward the kitchenette and called over her shoulder, "Please close the door."

Raina closed the front door and looked around for extra slippers. There wasn't any. She waited for a heartbeat, but Leilani didn't say it was okay for Raina to keep her shoes on. Chinese families rarely wore their outside shoes inside the house. Sighing inwardly, Raina took off her flip-flops and left them by the door.

Barefoot, she stepped into the tiny studio apartment. In front of her, several windows lined the opposite wall, including a sliding patio door that opened to a balcony. The white, vertical vinyl blinds were opened, letting in sunlight. The apartment was one long rectangle with a half wall that separated the bedroom space from the living room and kitchenette. The place was smaller than Raina's one-bedroom apartment in graduate school. As the Operations Manager, shouldn't Leilani get a bigger unit? But then again, Raina wouldn't complain either if she didn't have to pay rent or a mortgage.

Leilani closed the small refrigerator and handed Raina a bottle of water.

Raina held the cold bottle to her forehead. Why did the humidity make the heat feel so much worse? "You will not believe what happened last night."

Leilani stared back at Raina with flat, emotionless eyes.

Raina opened the bottle and took a long sip. What was with the look? Was Leilani too hungover to process what Raina just said? Or did she not care? This didn't make sense. Leilani had a deep sense of responsibility toward the family business. "Something terrible happened."

"Oookay," Leilani said. "Are you expecting me to beg you for the details?"

Raina snorted in disgust. What a cranky pants. She told her cousin what happened when the cooks opened the underground oven on the beach last night.

Leilani's eyes widened. She sagged against the wall and held onto the small refrigerator like her legs gave out from underneath her. "Who died?"

Raina shook her head. "Not a clue. Win drove Auntie May and Po Po to the police station a while ago."

"Did Tim show up?" Leilani asked.

Raina frowned. The name sounded familiar, but she couldn't place a face to it. "Who?"

"He's a detective."

"Ah, yes." Raina nodded. The plainclothes cop. The shady one that Auntie May had complained about before the ransom drop-off. "My husband doesn't like him. He contaminated the crime scene and didn't follow standard protocol."

"What does your husband know about standard protocol? Is he a cop?"

Raina cocked her head, studying her second cousin. Something felt off. "Yes, he is. That's why Auntie May wanted our help with the ransom drop-off."

Leilani stiffened. "I forgot. There are too many things going on. First, the kidnapping, and now this." She straightened, strode to the front door, and held it open. "I'm sorry, but right now is not a good time for a visit. I better get dressed and go find my grandma. Thanks for checking in on me."

Raina sipped the water, watching her cousin. She wasn't leaving until she got some answers for her trouble trekking through the forest. "When was the last time you spoke with your sister?"

"What?"

"Don't you think we need to find her and get the ransom money back? You were the one complaining about how everything is breaking down around here."

"I just can't right now. Let's worry about that later."

Raina's cell phone rang. She pulled it out of her purse and checked the display. "It's my grandma. She probably got news from the police." She accepted the call. "Hi, Po Po. Any news?"

Leilani crossed her arms and leaned against the doorframe, watching Raina.

"The victim is Leilani," Po Po said over the phone.

Raina blinked several times, trying to process what she had just heard. The police must have made a mistake. "Say that again?"

"I said the victim is Leilani," Po Po said.

"What's the news?" Leilani called out.

"Who's that?" Po Po said over the phone.

"I'm with Leilani at her apartment," Raina said into the phone. She covered the phone with her hands and addressed Leilani, "I'll tell you later."

"Oh my gosh," Po Po said over the phone. "The police must have gotten the twins mixed up."

"But they must have a reason for the assumption. Was there anything identifying her?" Raina said, trying to be vague. She didn't want Leilani to hear about her sister's death this way.

There was a shuffle over the phone, and then Auntie May came on the line.

"Did you say you're with Leilani?" Auntie May asked, her voice thick with emotion.

Raina cringed at Auntie May's brittle tone. She sounded hopeful and yet scared at the same time. If Raina were in Auntie May's position, it wouldn't matter which one of the twins died. It was still bad news all around. It was like asking someone to choose between their left hand or right hand. Just because someone had a dominant hand didn't mean this person was okay with losing the other one.

"Yes, do you want to talk to her?" Raina said.

"No, I'll talk to her when I get there," Auntie May said. "If I hear her voice now, I won't stop crying. I need to get myself under control first."

Raina hung up the phone and studied Leilani. She didn't want to deliver the bad news, but it might be better if her cousin was prepared for her grandma's visit. After all, this was her twin sister. No matter how much Leilani complained about her younger sister, the news would devastate her.

"Coz, you need to sit down for this," Raina said.

"It's my sister, isn't it?" Leilani said. Her voice broke at the end, and she took a shuddering breath. "What happened?" she whispered.

Raina swallowed the lump in her throat. "I'm sorry, Leilani. The victim in the imu was Ailani."

Leilani's round face crumpled. She slid onto the ground and wrapped her arms around her knees. A low keening wail filled the air.

Raina rushed over and wrapped her arms around her cousin. Even though she hadn't spent time with Ailani, Raina felt a wave of sadness wash over her. This death would break the Hawaiian branch of the Wong family.

The rift between the twins would never heal. Auntie May and Leilani would forever wonder if there was more they could have done to save Ailani. Why would someone kill her second cousin? And what happened to the ransom money?

9

AN OLD ALLY

When Auntie May showed up, Leilani fell into her grandma's arms. Auntie May and Leilani hugged, sobbing on each other's shoulders. Po Po caught Raina's gaze and jerked her head toward the door. Raina nodded. This wasn't the time to intrude. They left the apartment and closed the door quietly behind them. As Raina and Po Po made their way to the narrow entrance of the rainforest, a melancholy cloud seemed to hang over them.

When Po Po saw the tree canopy, she said, "This isn't a forest. It's a jungle. I hope there aren't any snakes in there." She shivered. "I hate snakes."

Raina strolled through the narrow opening between the two kukui trees. "It's more like a rainforest than a jungle because of the heavy tree canopy. Most of the animals are probably above us rather than at ground level. So, if there are any snakes, they are slithering around in the branches overhead."

Po Po grimaced at the thought. "Now that's comforting." She pulled a bright-red Taser out of her straw tote and pressed the button to turn it on. A loud crackle filled the air. "If any of those snakes fall down on me, I am zapping it."

Raina stared at the live Taser in horror. "How did you get that through the airport?"

Po Po gave her a Mona Lisa smile. "I have my ways."

Raina edged away from her grandma. "Don't come close to me. I don't want you to trip and accidentally zap me."

"I can go in front." Po Po waved the Taser in the air. "I'm ready to have me some fried snakes."

"Just stay on the path," Raina said from a few steps behind Po Po. What if her grandma accidentally zapped herself? Raina's stomach fluttered nervously at the thought. While her grandma was in good shape for her age, she was still a senior citizen. What if the zap caused a heart attack or a stroke? "Maybe I should hold the Taser? I don't want you to fall on it."

Po Po snorted. "Rainy, you're so clumsy, you'll zap yourself. I got this. Don't worry." She did a little jig. "I am light on my feet. I got twinkle toes." She stumbled on a tree root, and the Taser shot out of her hands.

Raina's eyes widened, and she forgot to breathe for a moment. "Po Po! Are you okay?" She grabbed her grandma's forearms and hauled her upright.

Po Po glared at the mangrove ferns on the side of the path. "Now that's a fine howdy doody."

Raina glanced at her grandma's hands. No Taser. She looked around the dirt path. No Taser. "What happened?"

Po Po pointed at the ferns. "The Taser fell in there."

The thick fern grove was as high as Raina's waist. She couldn't see any of the ground underneath it.

"I'm not going in there to get your Taser," Raina said. "All kinds of critters and bugs are probably in there. Look at all the spider webs."

"Or snakes," Po Po said with a shiver. "Forget it. I'll just get another one. Let's go."

Raina followed her grandma's lead.

"What do you think is going on at the resort?" Po Po asked. "Do you think Ailani's death was an accident?"

Raina shook her head. "No. The nightly show guaranteed that the body would be discovered within hours. This murder was premeditated."

Po Po was quiet for a moment, as if considering Raina's words. "I figured as much. Why would anyone want to kill Ailani?"

"We need to look into her lifestyle. She might have a long line of people who would want her dead. Look at how she treated her grandma and older sister. I can't believe she concocted a kidnapping scam to get money from the family."

"Maybe she needed it for an emergency."

"If it was a real emergency, they would have given her the money. There'd be no need for the ransom note and pickup. No, she was the black sheep of the family for a reason."

"I'm still holding out hope that she was a good kid."

Raina hoped her grandma was right. "Her last boyfriend was Detective Mars, but I'm not sure how we can approach him on this subject. It's not like he'll just want to chitchat with us about his love life."

"We need leverage. May said the police department had issues. Maybe we can talk to some of the locals and get some dirt."

"Actually, the best person to give us this information is probably Leilani. She dated him, too."

"I hate to bother Leilani at this time," Po Po said.

"Leilani is our best source for information. I want to leave her alone too, but her twin sister just died in mysterious circumstances. I'm sure she wants justice for her sister."

"You're right. She will help us."

They meandered in silence for several minutes, following the dirt path in the bumpy terrain and climbing over tree roots. Instead of the woodsy smell of home, the air was thick and damp. More earthy with the occasional whiff of rot. While Raina and Po Po were silent, the forest was a cacophony of trills, squawks, and clacks.

"Do you think Ailani's death has anything to do with the fake kidnapping and the ransom money?" Po

Po wondered out loud. She paused for a moment, hands on her hips, breathing hard.

Raina was glad her grandma decided they needed a break. The heavy air made the gentle stroll a lot more difficult than she remembered. If the death was accidental, why would the killer move the body to the underground oven at the beach? It made no sense. "What do you mean?"

Po Po raised an eyebrow. "Maybe she was coerced into the scam. What if there was a pimp or someone else involved in the background?"

Raina considered her grandma's words. It was within the realm of possibility. "But why kill Ailani? This person got the money, and Auntie May wasn't planning to pursue the matter further."

Po Po tapped her chin. "Or maybe the killing was a warning to May and had nothing to do with Ailani's scam."

Raina hadn't thought of this possibility. "If this was the case, wouldn't the killer threaten Auntie May first before actually taking action? And wouldn't she let us know about this threat?"

"Well, the developers have been bugging her to sell the property for years now. They could build a big fancy place on the twenty acres and charge premium prices for it. The property belonged to May's father, and she wanted to pass it down to the twins. We are talking about several million dollars here."

"We can ask Auntie May if she has gotten any

recent offers from developers. If they were pressuring her to sell, it'd make more sense to get to Leilani first. The older twin is the Operations Manager. She runs the place. Whereas, Ailani has nothing to do with the resort. Her death would have no impact on the resort."

"Maybe you're right," Po Po said with reluctance.

"Can your hacker get into Ailani's cell phone records? Maybe we can see who she contacted before her death," Raina said.

As the words left her mouth, Raina couldn't believe she no longer grappled with the morality of invading another person's privacy. Did this mean she had crossed some invisible line? Or maybe it was the exposure to social media, where it was assumed that privacy no longer existed?

Crash!

Raina jumped at the loud rustle behind them. She spun around, scanning the mangrove ferns in the underbrush and the branches overhead. Nothing.

Po Po pulled a slingshot out of her straw tote. She grabbed a kukui nut from the ground and loaded it on the slingshot. "What was that?"

Raina tightened the grip on her purse, her heart racing. Should she clap her hands and make a lot of noise? The park rangers at home said the noise would scare off bears. But there were no bears in Hawaii, right? "I don't know," she finally managed to squeak.

Po Po shot the nut into the underbrush at the base of the tree.

Thwack!

The nut disappeared into the mangrove ferns.

Squawk!

Five wild chickens burst out from the underbrush and flapped onto the path.

Raina's heart stopped for half a heartbeat and then resumed its normal speed.

The wild chickens shrieked and clucked, upset at the disturbance.

Po Po loaded her slingshot again and aimed at the birds.

Raina blocked the shot. "Leave them alone."

"We can grill them later for dinner at the beach."

The wild chickens fluffed out their feathers, making them appear bigger than they actually were. As they advanced toward Raina and Po Po, their mean beady eyes glistened with menace.

"Ya-ah!" Po Po dropped the nut, spun around, and took off.

The wild chickens cocked their heads in unison and squawked a challenge.

The fine hair on the back of Raina's neck stiffened. The chicken's robotic gesture was just too creepy. She held up her hands, exposing her palms, and bowed to the chicken. "You win."

The wild chickens broke eye contact and settled down to peck the ground.

Raina spun around and ran after her grandma. "Po Po! Wait up."

The terrain became uneven. Raina paused, glancing around. She didn't remember coming through this path the first time she went through the forest. Was she lost?

"Rainy, hurry up," Po Po called out. She was several feet ahead of Raina on the path.

With one final glance behind her at the wild chickens, Raina caught up to her grandma. They walked in silence for several minutes. Raina glanced around, hoping they were still on the right path. With the overhead canopy blocking out the remaining lingering sunlight, the forest was even spookier than before. Finally, they rounded a bend, and the path opened in front of them back to the staff apartment complex. This time they approached the area from the west side of the building.

Raina blinked several times and pulled out her cell phone to check the time. They had just been on a forty-minute walk that got them nowhere. When did they get turned around? When Po Po ran off? Or before then?

"Tell anyone about the wild chickens, and I'll disown you," Po Po said.

Raina gave Po Po a deadpan stare. "I wouldn't have to tell them anything. You'll probably tell people how you scared off the giant mutant chickens on a slow news day."

Po Po patted Raina's cheek fondly. "This is why you're my favorite."

Raina rolled her eyes. "Yeah, yeah. Everyone is your favorite. I'm calling Win to pick us up. I don't want to trek through the forest a third time today." She pulled out her cell phone and spoke to her younger brother. She hung up and turned to her grandma. "I'm surprised Win is okay with driving around in a minivan."

Po Po shrugged. "He can't say no to free. Besides"—she wiggled her eyebrows—"there's plenty of room for him and Jenny."

Raina groaned and covered her ears. "La-la-la. I don't want to think about this."

Po Po harrumphed. "Rainy, you have to let your hair down sometimes. If you want your husband begging for more, you got to get your super freak on." She gyrated her hips, popping one of them in the process.

Raina suppressed the urge to giggle. The words that came out of her grandma's mouth no longer shocked her. "Can we resume our discussion while we wait for our ride?"

Po Po paused mid-sway. "What were we talking about earlier? The chickens?"

"The twins," Raina said, glancing up at Leilani's window on the second floor. "You were going to contact your hacker friend to get into Ailani's phone records."

"Right," Po Po said. "This is why you're in charge, Sherlock. You don't get sidetracked like I do." She pulled out her phone and called her friend, strolling a few paces away for some privacy.

Raina's cell phone chirped at an incoming text message. It was an hour old and from a phone number she didn't recognize. She tapped on the icon.

THIS IS SONNY. I NEED TO TALK TO YOU. MALL FOOD COURT TOMORROW AT 9AM.

Her hand trembled. The only Sonny she knew had a silvery scar on the side of his face. He was also the Dai Lo of the Nine Dragons triad. The literal translation for Dai Lo was Big Brother, the formal title for the leader of a Chinese criminal organization. The last time Raina spoke with Sonny Kwan was several years ago, and she had almost lost her life in an explosion.

What was he doing here, and why did he want to see her all of a sudden? And most important of all, did she want to get tangled up in his dangerous world again?

10

A DISGUISE

When Win pulled the minivan into the gravel parking lot, Raina was done over-analyzing the text message from Sonny Kwan. She would tell Matthew about the message and let him handle it. That was what a husband was for—he could go out and slay the beast while she tended the fire. She had no problems with stereotypical roles—especially when it benefited her. Besides, her husband would have a heart attack if she met with the triad leader behind his back.

Po Po got off the phone and climbed into the passenger seat of the van. Raina got in and closed the sliding door in the back.

"My hacker friend is on it," Po Po said, turning around in her seat to address Raina.

Win pulled out of the parking lot. "What are you two hacking into now?"

"Ailani's cell phone records," Po Po said.

"Anything I can do to help?" Win asked.

Raina shot Po Po a look. She didn't want her younger brother involved in the murder investigation. The last time he had helped, he got into trouble that almost turned fatal. "Just focus on Jenny and driving us around."

Win rolled his eyes in the rearview mirror. "Fine. I'll butt out, but I need your help. I want to impress Jenny. Sweep her up in a vacation romance so that she wants to continue things when we both go back home."

Po Po rubbed her hands together with a beaming smile. "That is my specialty. I am in the business to impress."

"I'll need your help tomorrow. I planned a picnic next to a waterfall," Win said. "It has to be tomorrow. A storm is coming the following day, and it's supposed to be a big one."

Raina nodded. Everyone had been talking about this big one for a couple days already. She wasn't sure what to expect, but Auntie May wasn't preparing for it, so maybe it wasn't a big deal. She shifted her thoughts back to the schedule for tomorrow. Her brother better not expect Raina and Po Po to dress up in cheesy costumes or to serve as waitresses at the picnic. "Just tell us what you need later."

"By the way, Rainy, did you get Matthew's

message?" Win asked. "He has been looking all over the resort for you."

Raina shook her head and glanced at her phone. There were no voice messages or text messages from her husband. Undoubtedly, she would get the message later when she no longer needed the information. The reception for her cell phone company was horrible. "Do you know what he wanted?"

"I drove Matthew out to the airport," Win said. "He called me when I was at the beach with Jenny. He didn't tell me where he was going, but he took a backpack with him. I have a feeling he is not coming back tonight."

Raina gaped at her younger brother. She knew her honeymoon was over, but she didn't think she would spend the remaining time alone. She glanced at her cell phone again. Still no message from Matthew. She wasn't concerned about the state of their marriage, but she was concerned about her husband's physical safety. He was on crutches, for heaven's sake.

For Matthew to leave in such a hurry meant he was probably off doing something top-secret for the federal government again. Since he had left with a backpack, he obviously intended to return to help Raina with the rest of their luggage for the return trip home.

So, he probably flew into Honolulu, which was the hub for several federal departments in the Pacific Rim. Her husband had been grumbling about replacing Raina's fifteen-year-old car, so it didn't surprise her that he would take on a contract job to help with the down payment.

"It's Team Sherlock and Watson again," Po Po said with a fist pump in the air.

Her grandma had come to the same conclusion as Raina did about Matthew's sudden departure. As much as Po Po loved Matthew, she loved spending time alone with Raina even more. And whenever they investigated a case together, it took them back to a time when it was just the two of them.

"We don't need a man for this," Po Po said. "We got the brains, the beauty, and the brawn to take care of business on our own."

"Po Po, both of us are barely over five feet," Raina said. "We're lucky if we can take down a pygmy goat."

"Hey, what about me?" Win said. "I can be the brawn."

Raina caught the gleam in Po Po's eyes, and they both burst out laughing.

Win grunted and made the turn into the staff parking lot. Normally he dropped them off in front of the resort, but he was punishing them for laughing at him. The three of them trekked through the parking lot. Once Win went through the lobby, he made a beeline in the direction of the Wayfarer bar.

"Maybe we shouldn't have laughed at him," Raina said.

Po Po snorted. "Men and their fragile egos."

As Raina and Po Po strolled back to HQ, Raina told

her grandma about the text message from Sonny Kwan.

"I was hoping Matthew could take care of it," Raina said. The meeting with Sonny Kwan was early enough that they could help with the lunch date afterward. "But it looks like we'll have to figure something out ourselves."

"Don't worry. I have your back. I'll disguise myself and have my pepper spray ready. It's too bad I lost my Taser."

Raina gave her grandma a sideways glance. "No offense, but your scrawny muscles can't even scare off a hungry cat."

"Sonny hasn't harmed us yet. It should be fine," Po Po said. "Besides, I know his grandfather."

Raina didn't like the fluttery feeling in her stomach. Sonny Kwan was like Loki, unpredictable and an ally only when it suited him. And if she ignored his request to meet at the mall tomorrow, he would show up at the resort. He wasn't a man who took no for an answer.

Matthew's message finally came through right before dinner. Unfortunately, it revealed nothing more than what she had already guessed. And during the meal, she missed his call again, and when she called him back, the call went straight to voicemail. Raina tossed and turned all night. The next morning, her eyes were grainy, and she had a headache. She took some Tylenol, but it offered no relief.

As she brushed her teeth, Raina wondered why she felt out of sorts. She had accepted that her honeymoon was over. This wasn't an issue. With no children in the picture yet, she had plenty of alone time with Matthew at home. And since they were both workaholics at times, she understood why her husband left for Honolulu. No, her mood probably had nothing to do with him.

Did her mood have something to do with the murder investigation? Ailani was a family member, and though they weren't friends, Raina had always helped her family. It was her badge of honor—and her burden.

Or did Raina's mood have to do with the fact that she was a temporary guest? In her hometown, she had the resources and connections to find out about people's secrets. But, here on the island, the locals weren't going to trust her enough to talk about their deep, dark secrets.

And there was Sonny Kwan. Did the Nine Dragons triad have a branch here in Hawaii? The FBI had picked up the triad leader a few years ago, and Raina suspected he had struck a deal for his freedom. However, in the criminal underworld, alliances with the law were built in quicksand. It didn't mean they were still on the same side.

Raina shivered at a sudden thought. How did

Sonny track her down? Had he been keeping tabs on her all these years? Did he lure Matthew away to get to her?

It didn't matter. Raina had to get to the bottom of things. Her great-aunt was counting on her. And Po Po would be disappointed if Raina opted to stay on the sidelines for this investigation.

After a quick breakfast of oatmeal and coffee, Raina drove the minivan to the open-air mall. Po Po sat in the passenger seat, fiddling with the spy gear. When Raina parked, Po Po handed her the earpiece.

"The soundcheck went through fine," Po Po said. "And my hacker friend will be watching us through the video feed. If something goes wrong, he is calling the local cops."

Raina tucked the earpiece into her ear and shifted her hair to cover it. "Where is your hacker located?"

"I'm not sure," Po Po said. "I think he's in the Pacific Northwest somewhere."

"How did the two of you meet?"

Po Po considered Raina's question. "It's need-to-know, Rainy, and you don't need to know."

Raina suppressed the urge to roll her eyes. Her grandma often thought their little investigations were on par with the official channel. Raina had never considered herself more than a curious amateur. Most of the time, it felt like she stumbled on the killer through dumb luck more than anything else.

"Is your disguise ready?" Raina asked.

After dinner last evening, Po Po had gone out with Win to get a costume. Her grandma wanted to be incognito during the meeting with Sonny Kwan. Raina seriously doubted that a costume would help, but there was no arguing with her grandma when she had her heart set on something.

Po Po jerked a thumb at the big black trash bag on the rear passenger seat. "Just give me five minutes to change."

Raina glanced at the digital clock on the dashboard. They were fifteen minutes early. "I need to make a pit stop in the restroom. How will I recognize you?" She couldn't understand why her grandma didn't just wear a cheesy tourist outfit and a wig. Any other disguise would stand out in the crowd.

Po Po gave Raina a sly smile. "Oh, you won't be able to miss me."

Raina got out of the minivan, waved to her grandma, and took care of her business in the restroom. The entire spy charade with the earpiece and costume was only for her grandma's benefit. Sonny Kwan undoubtedly expected Po Po to make an appearance. He probably thought Matthew would listen in on the conversation too. Would this be enough to put the Triad leader on his best behavior?

11

FRIED CHICKEN

As Raina approached the food court, her eyes scanned the area. There! Sonny Kwan sat at one of the picnic tables to the right of the stage, facing the food court and watching the comings and goings. Next to him on the table were two coffee cups. The weak October sun reflected off the black designer sunglasses on his face. The mall had taken down the large shade canopy overhead, probably in preparation for the storm rolling in tomorrow.

For some reason, Raina had always assumed her meetings with the triad leader would be clandestine—and hidden from view. Why did he want such a public meeting? Was this a show for someone else? Would this put Raina in an awkward position she couldn't retreat from later?

Sonny slid his sunglasses down and peered over

them at Raina. He arched an eyebrow as if challenging her.

Raina had always thought of Sonny as the Chinese version of Fabio with his shoulder-length black hair tied into a ponytail at the nape of his neck. He wore a gray silk shirt and designer black jeans. The silvery scar on the side of his face added to his roguish pirate vibe.

She squared her shoulders and marched over. Sonny slipped his sunglasses back up and didn't bother hiding his smirk. When she sat across from him at the picnic table, he handed her a coffee cup like they were old pals meeting up for a chat.

"Don't drink the coffee," Po Po hissed in Raina's ear. "What if there's poison in it?"

Raina sniffed the coffee. Hazelnut-flavored Kona coffee. Yum. He knew her all too well. Now that was a scary thought. She took a sip of the warm beverage. If Sonny wanted her dead, he could do it without resorting to poison.

Po Po gasped in Raina's ear. "I can't believe you just did that."

Raina's gaze scanned the food court. Her grandma's comments were starting to be a distraction. She held the coffee cup close to her lips. "Stop talking," she mumbled into the smartwatch on her wrist.

"Did you say something?" Sonny asked. He removed his sunglasses and placed them on top of his head. His dark brown eyes studied Raina intently. Just because the man was a dangerous criminal, didn't mean he wasn't just as smart.

Raina cleared her throat. "I didn't say anything." She held up the cup. "Thanks for the coffee. I'm surprised you still remember what I like."

Sonny's lips curled in one corner. "It's been a few years, but you're quite memorable. It's too bad you picked Matthew Louie over me."

Raina's eyes widened. What did Sonny just say? While he might have flirted with her, and she had pretended to be his fiancée previously, it did not make them a former couple. It didn't even make them friends. "Why do you want to see me?"

"What happened to small talk? We haven't seen each other in years. Aren't you curious about what's been going on in my life?"

Raina snorted. "You can't tell me the truth, or you'll have to kill me. And I don't want to hear the lies, so let's just get down to business."

Sonny burst out laughing. "And this is why you're the woman of my dreams."

"I said I don't want to hear any lies. Get on with it."

Still smiling, Sonny said, "I'm trying to find your cousin, Ailani Wong."

Raina choked on the coffee. She pulled a tissue out of her purse and dabbed at her mouth and shirt. Her cousin just died, and Sonny was looking for her. This couldn't be a coincidence. Raina should play along and pretend Ailani was still alive. Maybe he could offer a clue as to why someone would want her cousin dead. "Why are you looking for her?"

"It's better if you don't know."

Raina gave him a deadpan stare. Really? Another need-to-know comment? First, her husband. Then, her grandma. And now, Sonny. What was going on here? Had she lost her sleuthing mojo? When had people stopped trusting her?

"Then you don't need to know either," Raina said. "I'm not handing over my cousin to you. She's better off not getting involved in whatever you're up to."

Sonny wagged his index finger, tsking the entire time. "I'm not the bad guy, remember? And your cousin has information about a local gambling ring."

Raina sipped her coffee, letting the silence drag out. Sonny was out to take care of Sonny. At his level, he had too many enemies and too many ties to leave the family business. Organized crime wasn't something he could walk away from like he would a career change. And his definition of bad guy might be different from hers. "I don't trust you."

Sonny clutched his heart as if in pain. "You sure know where to point that dagger." He smiled. "I like it."

Po Po chuckled in the earpiece. "Me too."

Raina jumped at the sound. She had forgotten that her grandma was listening in on the conversation. Where was she? And in what disguise? Raina glanced around the food court but didn't see anyone resembling her grandma.

Sonny gave Raina a puzzled look. "Are you okay?"

Raina nodded. "Just a mosquito bite."

Someone dressed in a chicken costume came around the fried chicken hut and held a tray of samples.

Raina hoped the person would come close enough so she could nab a sample of the Filipino fried chicken. It would be even better if the sample was dipped in gravy. She squinted at the square mesh in the chicken breast but couldn't make out the face inside the costume.

The person began to hand the paper Dixie cups to random shoppers.

Raina dismissed the chicken costume. There was no way her grandma's pride would allow her to pretend to be a food mascot, especially after her encounter with the flock of wild chickens in the rainforest.

"I can't help you," Raina said, returning her attention to Sonny.

"Why not?" Sonny asked.

"Because Ailani is dead."

Sonny gaped at Raina. "What happened?"

Raina told him about finding the body at the luau and Auntie May identifying it.

"I'm sorry for your loss," Sonny said stiffly.

Raina nodded and blinked rapidly at the sudden tears in her eyes. Why was she crying? And especially in front of Sonny? She wasn't close to her second cousin, but she felt horrible for Auntie May.

"What is Ailani's home address?" Sonny asked.

"I don't know," Raina said.

"Can you ask your great-aunt or your other cousin?"

Raina shook her head. "I'm not helping you. You have the wrong person for the job." She hadn't thought about searching Ailani's apartment, but it made perfect sense. And she had better take a quick look before other people got the same idea. Did her cousin's death have anything to do with this illegal gambling ring? Gambling was illegal in Hawaii—even bingo fit into this category.

The person in the chicken costume approached them and held out a Dixie cup. "Want a sample of our fried chicken?"

Raina gaped at the chicken mascot. That was Po Po's voice coming out of the chicken costume. Wow. Did they run out of costumes at the shop?

Sonny glared at the chicken costume. "You're interrupting a critical conversation. Get out of here, or you'll regret it."

Raina shivered at the chill in his voice. "She's just doing her job." She took the Dixie cup. "Thank you. But you better leave."

The person inside the chicken costume flapped a wing. Probably to give Sonny the finger.

Raina stood. "I have to go. It was nice catching up with you, but I don't want to see you again."

"I thought we were friends," Sonny said slowly.

Raina wasn't going to let the man guilt trip her into agreeing to help him. "Even though my great-aunt and cousin have been estranged from Ailani for a while, they are devastated by her death. I will be busy making arrangements and running errands for them. Good luck with whatever you're doing, but please, leave me and my family out of it."

"Wait!" Sonny held out his hand as if to stop her.

Po Po tossed the tray of chicken samples onto Sonny's lap and whipped out her pepper spray.

Sonny glared at the chicken mascot. He opened his mouth—

Po Po blasted Sonny in the face.

"No!" Raina called out. She wasn't sure if she was talking to Sonny or to her grandma. She didn't want the situation to escalate.

Sonny jerked and covered his face with his hands. He screamed a string of curse words in both Chinese and English.

Po Po grabbed Raina's arm and pushed her toward the parking lot, dropping tiny glass vials on the ground.

Ping! Ping! Ping!

The little glass vials shattered on the concrete, leaving wet splatters where they made contact. Po Po's special stink bombs. There was a heartbeat of silence and then skunk funk filled the air, followed by rotting kimchi and the hot burn of chili peppers. It was a small wonder the air didn't change into a radioactive green cloud.

Raina blinked rapidly, but tears streamed down her face unheeded. She swallowed the bile in the back of her throat, having been through this routine before. Breathing through her mouth didn't help. How in the world did her grandma get her weapons of mass destruction through the airport security?

Sonny gagged, clutching at his throat. His eyes glowed red from the irritation from the pepper spray. He tried to stand but stumbled.

Pandemonium broke out among the shoppers. People ran away from the food court, while others ran toward it. The noise level increased until several people were shouting.

As Raina ran after her grandma, she turned around and called out, "I'm sorry. My grandma's crazy. No one can control her."

With tears streaming from his eyes, Sonny cupped his hands around his mouth and shouted, "Rainy, you owe me for this. You better have the address when I come to collect later."

When they were back at the minivan, Raina put the pedal to the metal. She hightailed it out of the parking lot like someone had released the flying monkeys from the basement. She didn't know if Sonny had other associates watching their tête-à-tête, but she wasn't taking any chances. And it wouldn't take long for Sonny to recover and come after them.

Po Po pulled off the chicken mascot head and laughed. "Now that was fun."

As Raina rounded the corner in the minivan, a fire engine pulled into the mall parking lot. A police vehicle, with its lights flashing and sirens blaring, passed Raina on the opposite lane.

"You better tell your hacker friend to erase the video feed," Raina said. "If the cops find you, I think you're going to jail."

"He's the one who called nine-one-one. He probably thought we couldn't handle Sonny," Po Po said with pride in her voice. She glanced up from her smartphone, her eyes gleaming. She was enjoying the mayhem a little too much for Raina's taste. "But that's a good suggestion." Her fingers flew across her screen as she tapped out the message.

"What were you thinking?" Raina asked.

Po Po shrugged. "I thought he was going to grab you. I just followed my gut instinct."

Raina snorted. She wasn't surprised her grandma's gut instinct had to do with her stink bombs. Raina's thoughts drifted back to her meeting with Sonny. He knew where she was staying and her family members, which meant he had been doing surveillance on her movements for a while. Why hadn't she noticed this? She shivered at the thought of her next encounter with the triad leader—when he came to collect.

12

KNOCK ME OUT

P o Po tapped on the screen of her smartphone. Her eyes widened, and her voice came out tight. "The emergency room. The boy fell off his jet ski and bumped his head."

Raina groaned inwardly. Her brother wasn't someone who did stupid things to impress a girl—or at least he hadn't in the past. "If he remembered to message you, he's probably okay."

"He didn't message me. Jenny posted a picture of Win falling off the jet ski on social media."

Raina pulled over and searched for the local hospital on the GPS. After making her selection, she signaled and pulled back into traffic. "When did the two of you become friends on the Internet?"

"We aren't really friends, Rainy," Po Po said, glancing up from her phone. "I'm more of an undercover spy. If that girl wants to spend time with my grandchildren, I need to make sure she's A-OK."

"I thought Jenny passed the test at brunch a couple days ago."

"I consider that more of an initial screening," Po Po said. "Next, I'll have Lucy run a background check on Jenny. I'll continue to stalk her on social media."

Lucy Fong was Po Po's unofficial foster granddaughter who ran a private investigation office in the California town of Morro Cliff Village. She had access to databases that were only available to her profession. Luckily, she was always more than willing to help out Po Po. In some ways, she spoiled Po Po rotten.

Raina gave her grandma a sideways glance. "Po Po, you scare me sometimes."

"Hey, I just want to make sure we don't end up with a serial killer in the family. And if she posted it, then it's public knowledge. I am not doing anything I shouldn't be doing."

"Jenny is Win's first real girlfriend," Raina said. There was no use reasoning with her grandma, but she had to try for her brother's sake. "Don't you think we should wait and see before we scare her off?"

Po Po pretended to consider Raina's words. "Yeah... no. I go straight for the jugular when it comes to my family."

Raina's thoughts drifted back to what happened with Sonny Kwan at the food court. Yep, straight for the jugular, all right. She had no doubt that Sonny would come looking for her at the resort. Or maybe he would come looking for her grandma. Great. Now Raina had to keep an eye out for Sonny and keep him away from her grandma. While he might not kill Po Po, Raina had a feeling he might get even. "Sonny isn't a forgiving man."

Po Po swallowed audibly. "You have a point there. I know how to make myself scarce."

Raina turned into the hospital parking lot. "I forgot to ask. What's up with the chicken mascot costume?"

Po Po unbuckled her seat belt and opened her car door. "It was either that or Pokémon. Apparently, they have a very limited selection here. With Halloween only a couple weeks away, you'd think there would be more stock. Even my costume closet at home has a bigger selection than the shop's racks." She grinned, then added, "I offered the fried chicken manager fifty dollars to hand out samples for him. Speaking of chicken, Filipino fried chicken is yummy. He even gave me extra gravy."

Raina turned off the car engine. "When did you eat? How come you didn't save me some?"

Po Po shrugged. "It's not my fault you took so long in the bathroom."

They got out of the car, and Raina turned on the alarm to lock the minivan. The drizzle earlier turned into a steady downpour. Unlike the rain at home, the air was warm and slightly muggy. Most of the locals still wore shorts and sandals and went about their business like it was a sunny day. Raina and Po Po tucked their heads under their rain jackets and power walked to the entrance of the emergency room.

The receptionist directed them to a triage area. They found Win with a bandaged arm on the hospital bed in one of the consulting rooms, which was more like a cubicle than an actual room. Even with the teal curtain pulled open, the twelve-by-ten-foot space was just big enough for a hospital bed, an IV drip system, and a chair.

"What are you two doing here?" Win asked. Strands of black hair escaped from his unruly man bun. The scruff on his face looked even worse under the fluorescent lights and against the gray painted walls.

"Jenny posted about what happened to you on her social media," Raina said. "We came by to check on you."

"Where is your girlfriend?" Po Po asked.

"Will you stop calling her that? Jenny is not my girl-friend," Win said, sounding completely defeated.

Po Po arched an eyebrow at Raina, who shrugged in return.

Raina wondered if the two of them broke up already. This would be his shortest relationship ever.

"Okay—your friend," Po Po said. "Where is your friend?"

"Jenny went to get me something to drink," Win said. "I'm waiting for the doctor to come back for a final check. I have a concussion, and he wants to make sure I'm okay before sending me home." Win glanced at his watch. "Only fifteen minutes left to wait."

"What is wrong with your arm?" Po Po asked.

"I got a cut about five inches long," Win said. "I don't even remember what I scratched it on. It will probably give me a manly scar though." His face turned a deep red. "I guess you can't take the nerd outside and expect him to morph into an outdoor adventurer."

Raina reached for her brother's hair, hoping to ruffle it. The poor boy was trying too hard.

Win batted Raina's hand away and scowled at her. "Rainy, stop it. I'm not a child anymore."

Jenny returned to the consulting room with a bottle of iced tea. "Win, I can't find any water, but I hope you're okay with iced tea." She appeared startled when she noticed Raina and Po Po next to her boyfriend. "Oh, hi. It wasn't my fault. I told him it was a bad idea to get on the jet ski. The water was too choppy."

The young brunette towered over Raina and Po Po. Her damp hair was matted against her head and had sand in it. Despite her deep tan, she looked washed out under the fluorescent hospital lights. Or maybe she was afraid Win's family would freak out about his injury.

Po Po gave Jenny a reassuring smile. "No one is blaming you, dear."

"Oh, okay," Jenny said, with relief written all over her face.

A nurse stuck her head into the consulting room. "Only one person can be with the patient back here. The rest of you have to go to the waiting area."

Po Po settled herself more comfortably on the plastic chair. She arched an eyebrow as if challenging Raina and Jenny to dislodge her. Like anyone would dare try.

"See you on the other side, Win," Raina said, no longer concerned about his physical safety. If he was more upset about looking like a fool in front of his girl-friend then he was fine.

Jenny gave Win the plastic iced tea bottle and followed Raina to the waiting area. She sat down on a metal folding chair, twisting the bottom of her cover-up wrap around her finger.

Raina took the seat next to Jenny and glanced around the waiting area. The decor was bare bones, no magazines or fake plants. Several rows of metal folding chairs under the fluorescent lights. It was a temporary space to get the family members out of the way until their patients either got sent home or got checked into the hospital for a longer stay. Most of the people wore anxious expressions on their faces, glancing up at anyone's entrance and then returning to scroll mind-lessly on their phones.

"What happened this morning?" Raina whispered. She didn't want to come off as grilling the younger woman, but she wasn't comfortable with sitting in silence.

Win and Jenny were in that awkward, yet all-consuming, beginning stage of a new relationship. Jenny probably wanted minimal interactions with Win's family. Raina didn't blame Jenny one bit for this. After all, a vacation romance wasn't all that fun when you add in family members.

Jenny curled a strand of brown hair behind her ear, exposing a red birthmark on her neck, underneath the earlobe. It was the size of a thumbprint. She probably wore her long hair loose to hide it. "Win has been acting weird all morning. All of a sudden, he transformed into an outdoor adventure type." She gave Raina a sheepish look. "But we both know he prefers role-playing games on the computer. So when Jonathan wanted to get on the jet skis—"

"Who is Jonathan?" Raina asked. Another person was involved in the accident?

Jenny's blue eyes lit up. "Someone we've been hanging out with by the rental shack. Jonathan is definitely the outdoors type."

Raina nodded in understanding. The romantic rival. No, not a rival. Win had probably never even left the friend zone. Maybe her brother sensed something was off with the budding relationship, which explained this sudden mulish need to ride a jet ski in the choppy water. "So my brother fell off the jet ski?"

"Yes, and a wave pushed the jet ski on top of him."

Jenny's face turned ashen. "That was a very scary moment. I'm glad he had on a life vest. He was lucky that Jonathan is a strong swimmer, and he carried Win up the beach. He saved Win's life."

Raina groaned inwardly. Her brother was carried like a damsel in distress? No wonder he was in such a cranky mood. "Everything is okay now. My family has a knack for attracting danger. The weather is turning, so Win will probably not spend as much time in the water for the rest of our trip."

Maybe the family made too big of a deal over Jenny during brunch. Raina didn't want her brother to get hurt, so she was hoping a new girlfriend would distract him from the murder investigation. But now, it looked like the murder investigation would distract him from the girl. Just because the feelings were one-sided, didn't mean the rejection hurt any less. And since Win was also Leilani's cousin, he might as well get on the amateur sleuth bus like everyone else in the family.

Raina changed the subject. Done was done. There was no point in dwelling on the jet ski accident. "Do you feel better after visiting...your sister?"

A strange emotion flashed across Jenny's face, but Raina didn't know how to describe it—pain, fear, or guilt? Raina blinked. The younger woman looked nervous again.

As Jenny spoke, the glow faded from her blue eyes. "Every single day, I wish Sarah were still alive. I thought after all these years the pain would disappear by now."

"My dad died fifteen years ago, and I still miss him terribly," Raina said. The strange emotion earlier on Jenny's face had to be a trick of the fluorescent light. She was brokenhearted about her older sister's death. "The pain never disappears, but it gets easier, especially when you fill it with love for the people in your life. How old were you when your sister died?"

"I was in the third grade," Jenny said. "It was Sarah's last year in high school. She had two best friends, and the three of them were inseparable. One of the friends broke up with her boyfriend, so all three of them decided to do a girls' night out for homecoming. I don't remember why, but I think Sarah's boyfriend couldn't go for some reason."

Raina hesitated. Would it sound morbid to ask for more details? "You said she died from a car accident? What happened?"

"The driver hit a tree. My sister flew out the backseat and into a ravine. She wasn't wearing a seatbelt."

Raina hoped Jenny's sister didn't suffer before her death. What a horrible way to go. "Do you think things would have turned out differently if Sarah had gone to the homecoming dance with her boyfriend?"

"My sister would probably still be alive," Jenny said, her voice tight with anger. "All three of them had double the blood alcohol limit. They shouldn't have been on the road that night."

"I'm sorry."

Jenny nodded, and they lapsed into silence.

Raina's mind was racing. She wondered what had happened afterwards. Did the driver do jail time? Was the accident the catalyst that had caused Jenny's parents to divorce and move to the Big Island?

She gave Jenny a sideways glance. The younger woman had pulled out her cell phone and hunched over. There was an invisible "do not disturb sign" in the space between them. Raina's window for asking questions had officially closed.

Raina's cell phone rang. She pulled it out of her purse and glanced at the screen. It was from Matthew. What awful timing. She would rather talk to Jenny than her husband. He would only tell Raina it was "need-to-know," and she didn't need to know any details. Who wanted to hear that again? But she missed him, and it would be nice to hear his voice. She turned to Jenny. "Sorry, it's my husband. I need to take this call."

Jenny nodded. She pressed her lips into a thin line as if clamping down on her story. Maybe she regretted how much personal information she had shared with a stranger. There was no doubt her sister's death was just as raw today as it was in Jenny's childhood.

Raina tapped on the screen to accept the call. "Give me a second, hon."

She got up, strolled to the sliding glass doors, and stepped outside to the covered breezeway that led to the main hospital building. "When are you coming back?"

"I have a flight booked for tonight," Matthew said.

Raina glanced up at the gray overcast sky. "Okay. Be careful. The rain is starting to get worse here."

"If it gets too bad, the airport will cancel the flight. Is everything okay?"

Raina brought him up to date on the murder investigation and Win's jet ski accident. She hesitated. Should she tell him about her meeting with Sonny Kwan?

"What else happened?" Matthew asked. "I know you're holding back on me."

Raina sighed inwardly. When did her husband become a mind reader? She told him about her meeting with Sonny Kwan.

Matthew cursed over the phone. "Sonny was supposed to be in Honolulu. He's the reason I came over here."

Raina's eyes widened. She didn't bother asking her husband for more details because he wouldn't give them to her. "Are we on the same side with Sonny? Can I trust him?"

Even as the questions left Raina's mouth, she realized they were naïve questions. If Sonny could be trusted, he wouldn't have left her husband high and dry on another island when they were supposed to work together.

"At the moment, but I'm not sure for how long," Matthew said.

"Sonny wants Ailani's address, and he thinks I can get him the information. He will come looking for me soon."

Matthew cursed again. He was becoming a little bit of a potty mouth. Or maybe this was a side of him that Raina never knew about. Maybe he was letting it all hang out now that the honeymoon was over.

"Are you okay, hon?" Raina asked. "Is your foot bothering you?"

"I left the pain meds in the hotel room," Matthew said. "I guess you can tell I'm not in the best of moods."

"I still miss you though."

They blew air kisses and hung up. Raina stared at the phone for a second longer and slipped it back into her purse. She glanced up at the gray overcast sky again. Matthew was a smart man. If the weather got worse, he should know better than to get on a tiny island hopper plane.

13

LOST AND FOUND

An hour later, the four of them were back at the main building of the resort. Win and Jenny went to the elevator to return to their rooms upstairs. Raina and Po Po crossed the lobby, and Po Po knocked on the locked door next to the concierge counter.

Auntie May opened the door and waved them inside. "Come in." She closed and locked the door behind them.

The office was about sixteen-by-sixteen feet and held two desks and a bank of filing cabinets. There were no windows in the room other than the large one-way mirror window that looked out to the comings and goings in the lobby. The walls were painted a pale peach. Several potted indoor plants were scattered throughout the room, on top of filing cabinets and side tables. The blanket hanging off the arm of the recliner in the corner indicated it was used regularly for nap time.

Raina was surprised to see Auntie May was already back at work. She glanced at the spreadsheet on the computer monitor—her great-aunt was dealing with payroll. Okay, maybe not so big of a surprise after all. Raina had grown up surrounded by small business owners, and she knew that, rain or shine, employees needed to be paid. Should she volunteer to help take some of the load off her great-aunt's frail shoulders?

"Do you need anything?" Auntie May asked, settling back into her swivel chair.

Po Po took the recliner, leaving the other swivel chair for Raina. "Tell Auntie May what you need, Sherlock."

Raina settled into the chair, flushing. She hated it when Po Po made it sound like she was some kind of hotshot detective. Sometimes it felt like her grandma was setting the bar a little too high. What if Raina fell on her face?

"Have there been any offers to purchase the resort recently?" Raina asked.

Auntie May shook her head. "The last serious buyer lost interest when they realized my parents established a separate trust to protect the rain forest area. It's a no-build zone."

Po Po's theory that developers were pressuring the family to sell was no longer valid. Ailani's death probably didn't have anything to do with the resort at all.

"Auntie May, we would like to search Ailani's apartment," Raina said. "Can you give us her address? Do you have a spare key?"

"I need to clean out her apartment before the end of the month, but I just can't do it," Auntie May said.

"We'll do it for you," Po Po said. "We'll box everything up and bring it back to the resort."

They discussed what things to keep and what things to donate and throw out.

Auntie May wrote down Ailani's address on a sticky note and handed it to Raina. "I don't have a spare key, but Leilani probably has one."

"Where is Leilani?" Po Po asked.

"She is at the restaurant, talking to the repair person," Auntie May said. "The walk-in freezer is broken again."

"Let me keep you company for a bit," Po Po said, then turned to Raina. "Come get me when you have the key."

Raina left the office and strode across the lobby to the Wayfarer restaurant. The hostess greeted Raina and asked if she wanted a table or booth. Raina introduced herself and asked for her cousin Leilani.

The hostess jerked a thumb at the bar. "She's with Big Mac right now."

Raina thanked the hostess. As Raina strode into the bar, her stomach growled. It was almost two o'clock in the afternoon—a long time since breakfast.

Big Mac and Leilani, heads bent together, were

chatting at the bar. Her cousin's stocky figure was squeezed into a muumuu with turquoise turtles printed on the fabric. Her brown eyes appeared anxious and continuously scanned the room. There were a handful of customers seated at the bar tables and watching the TV. With the bad weather forcing the tourists indoors, Raina had expected the bar to be more crowded.

Raina strode up to them and took the seat next to Leilani. "Hi, Coz." She tipped her chin at Big Mac.

Leilani turned to Raina with a tight smile. "We're in the middle of a private conversation right now."

Big Mac studied Leilani from the corner of his eyes, almost as if he was afraid of her.

Raina didn't know what was going on, but she didn't like this version of her cousin. "Then go someplace private to have it. I need to talk to you. It's important. It has to do with your sister's death."

Big Mac dropped the glass tumbler in his hand. It shattered on the floor. "Ailani's dead?"

Leilani stiffened, and when she spoke, her voice was tight with anger. "Please respect my family's privacy. I don't want to discuss this in public."

"Auntie May asked us to look into it," Raina said. "Do you think I want to play armchair detective on my honeymoon?"

"How did Ailani die?" Big Mac asked.

Leilani ignored him again. "I think you're one of those busybody types who sticks her nose in everyone's business. It probably makes you feel special or something."

Raina frowned in confusion. She understood that sometimes people lashed out in their grief, but this was ridiculous. She softened her voice. "Let's not fight anymore, Leilani. We're on the same team. Both of us want to find out who killed your sister and to keep the resort going."

"What's going on here?" Big Mac asked again, this time raising his voice.

Raina and Leilani both turned and glared at Big Mac. Both women hopped off the barstool and grabbed an empty table far enough from the bar to prevent eavesdropping.

"When Auntie May got the ransom note for Ailani, she begged my grandma for help," Raina said. "She thought the local police wouldn't be able to help her."

"Why you? Why not a private investigator or someone more professional?"

Raina stared at her cousin in confusion. "Did you bonk your head or something?"

"No, why?"

"Nevermind. You just seem forgetful."

"It's the stress. You were saying?"

"My husband is a homicide detective, and my grandma and I have solved a few murders at home."

"I see." Leilani licked her lower lip. "I didn't think my grandma cared all that much about what happened to the spare granddaughter."

"There are no such things as a spare when it comes to family. Just because you have a dominant hand doesn't mean you're okay with losing the other one. Family is family. It doesn't matter what happened, but you can always come home."

"Do you really believe that, Rainy?"

"Yes, I do. Your family are the people who love you. So there is no shame in apologizing and coming home. And in some cases, you don't even need to apologize. Just come home."

"That's easy for you to say. You're not a screw-up."

Raina snorted. "I have also been the black sheep in the family, but I never doubted that my family loves me." She told Leilani what happened when her grandfather had left her three million dollars to distribute to his secret family and the fallout with her cousins. "Even family can have differing opinions, but you need to have faith that it will work out. And to just keep showing up."

Leilani studied Raina thoughtfully for a long moment. Her eyes filled with tears, and she blinked several times to get rid of them.

Raina thought her cousin's reaction was slightly excessive. Hadn't she always been the good twin? The responsible one?

"Sorry for calling you a nosy busybody," Leilani finally mumbled.

"Don't worry about it. I have been called worse.

Now, can you answer a few questions about your sister?"

Leilani raised an eyebrow, smirking. "You're that easy, huh?"

Raina gave her cousin a cheeky grin. "I don't believe in playing hard to get."

Leilani burst out laughing. "All right, what do you want to know?"

"Do you have a spare key to Ailani's apartment?"

Leilani pulled out a set of keys from her pocket, removed a key, and placed it on the table. She kept her finger on top of the key. "Why do you want to search my sister's apartment? What are you hoping to find?"

"I have no idea what we will find. I guess I'm just trying to look into Ailani's lifestyle and figure out why anyone would want to kill her. Do you know if she has a long-standing feud with anyone or if she has offended anyone recently?"

"I guess offending me and grandma doesn't count. What about that boyfriend of hers, Detective Mars? With all the rumors of cronyism and favoritism at the department, I have a feeling he might be up to his armpits in filth."

"What do you know about an illegal gambling ring in Kauai?" Raina asked. She wondered why Leilani wanted the detective investigated. Was it a personal vendetta to cause trouble for the detective, or did he have something to do with the illegal activities?

"Try an illegal gambling ring across all the islands in Hawaii."

Raina's eyes widened. For some naïve reason, she had always assumed this was paradise. She didn't realize there was a dark underbelly to the sunshine, beach, and tourists. "Tell me more."

"The Nine Dragons triad controls them. They were originally from Toronto but have branches around the world. They even have layers of shell corporations, which make them pseudo-legal. That is the situation here. A shell corporation runs an "entertainment business"—Leilani made air quotes with her fingers—"A lot of the local politicians and even law enforcement have their hands in this honeypot. Sometimes through political donations or they are actually some of the people organizing it."

Raina hesitated. Should she tell Leilani about Sonny Kwan? Raina felt oddly protective about the triad leader. After her conversation with her husband, she was more convinced than ever that Sonny was a double agent in his criminal organization. The more people who knew about him, the higher the chances he would be found out, which in turn could endanger Raina's husband. "Do you think Ailani is involved with this entertainment business?"

Leilani took a long sip of her cocktail, mulling over Raina's question. She sighed. "This will come out eventually. She's their local bookkeeper."

Raina gaped at her cousin. "Are you kidding me?"

"You think criminals don't have to deal with accounting, expenses, and payroll?"

"Actually, it has never crossed my mind. I thought maybe they walk around with bags of cash in gym bags."

Leilani snorted. "Maybe back in the last century. These people are smart and hide their trails. Dead people can't talk, after all."

"Is that why they killed Ailani? She knew too much?"

The corner of Leilani's mouth twisted like she was smiling to herself. "They wouldn't dare touch Ailani. They knew she regularly backed up the account numbers and names somewhere. They'd figured Ailani was too deep into the scheme to betray them or pull herself out."

"The federal government probably needs to charge them for tax evasion or something similar like they did with Al Capone to get him behind bars," Raina said. This explained why Sonny was looking for Ailani. "Do you think Ailani was killed for working with the feds? Or appearing to work for the feds?"

"I don't think so. Ailani wasn't a snitch."

"If Ailani had a job, why would she need to extort money from her family?"

Leilani slid the key across the table. "What if she needed the money to purchase her freedom off the island? Maybe she was done with working for sleazeballs."

Raina raised an eyebrow. "If that is the case, why didn't she just ask for the money? There's no need to sneak around to get it. Auntie May probably would have given it to Ailani willingly. Heck, even my grandma would have given Ailani the money willingly if that was the case."

Leilani looked abashed. "Maybe Ailani has cried wolf one too many times, and she was afraid no one would listen this time."

Raina considered Leilani's words. It was strange to hear her cousin defending her sister. But, in the end, the bond between the twins was stronger than anything else. Or was this survivor's guilt? Maybe her cousin felt guilty for all the negative things she said about her sister. And now, Leilani was trying to rewrite the memory of Ailani's personality?

Big Mac came over, placing two Leilani cocktails on the table. He stood next to the table and crossed his arms. "I am not leaving until you answer my questions."

Leilani finished the rest of her cocktail, leaving only the wedge of lemon and ice behind. She stood. "I have things to do." She paused and gave Raina a tight-lipped smile. "Thanks, Coz. You just made my day with this chat. Let me know what else I can do to help."

"Wait!" Big Mac grabbed Leilani's forearm, and she brushed him off. She fled the bar without a backward glance.

Raina took a sip of the Leilani cocktail and

grimaced. The bartender had given her extra vodka. She would have to pretend to sip the drink, or she might slide off the barstool later. The hint of lychee and green tea flavor was just as refreshing as before. She was surprised her cousin didn't have a taste before leaving.

Big Mac swiveled his attention to Raina. "Tell me what's going on, or do I need to add some pressure?"

Raina rolled her eyes. She wasn't afraid of him, at least not at the bar where there were several sets of eyes watching them. Besides, they looked as if they were about the same weight. She might be able to push him over in a fight.

His thick, blond hair was pulled back in a ponytail as usual, but it didn't have its usual sheen. His Arctic blue eyes were as cold as ever, but he looked as if something was bothering him.

"As Leilani said, this is private family business," Raina said. "But I'm willing to talk if properly incentivized."

Big Mac flicked a glance at the drink in front of Raina. "That's on the house. If you want, I can give you another one."

Raina gave him a deadpan stare. "I'm not much of a drinker, and this is more poison than pleasure for me. How about this—you answer a question for me, and I will answer a question for you? Tit for tat. What do you say?"

Big Mac licked his lower lip nervously. "Okay."

Raina took another small sip of the cocktail. She had to ask open-ended questions so that the bartender would keep talking. Yes or no questions would end the interview faster than she wanted. "How would you describe your relationship to Leilani?"

"We're not in a relationship."

"I didn't say you were. I said to describe your relationship to my cousin." Raina tapped on her cocktail glass. "I know it is not a simple boss-and-employee relationship. After all, you named a drink after her."

Big Mac grabbed the other Leilani drink and took a long gulp. "Fine. This stays between the two of us."

Raina nodded eagerly and leaned in for some juicy gossip.

"I have been in love with Leilani since high school. At the time, I was casually dating her best friend."

"I'm assuming the best friend is now out of the picture?"

Big Mac hesitated and then nodded reluctantly.

"Then what is stopping you from pursuing Leilani?"

"It's complicated."

"Because she is your boss?"

Big Mac chuckled. "That is the least of it."

"Explain it to me. Maybe I can help."

"My high school girlfriend died in a car accident during homecoming night."

Raina paused mid-sip, her mind whirling until

several things snapped into place. "Was her name Sarah Harris?"

Big Mac blinked. "How...did you know Sarah?"

Raina shook her head. "Her younger sister, Jenny, told me about Sarah."

This explained Big Mac's reluctance to confess his feelings to Leilani. Her cousin would undoubtedly reject him because she had survived a car accident that her best friend didn't. Getting together with him would constantly remind her of this painful memory.

In addition, Leilani could easily steal alcohol from the bar. Did she encourage underage drinking? Was Leilani the driver or passenger? And what role did Ailani play in the car accident?

"Hey," Big Mac said. "It's your turn to give me info."

Raina shifted her attention back to the bartender. She told him that Auntie May had identified the body at the luau. She didn't go into detail about what she had learned from Leilani. As Raina spoke, her gaze settled on Leilani's empty cocktail glass. It held a wedge of lemon. Raina's gaze shifted to the swirl of yellow, peach, and hint of light purple in her glass. Her voice trailed off. Something was off about the drinks.

Big Mac snapped his fingers in front of Raina's face. "Hey!"

Raina blinked, focusing on his face. "Sorry, I..." She pointed at the empty cocktail glass. "What did you make for Leilani?"

Big Mac's gaze followed Raina's finger. He frowned in confusion. "Her usual."

Raina shook her head and pointed to his drink. "That's her usual. She told me that she only drinks the Leilani here at the bar." She swiveled her finger back at the empty glass. "Wasn't that a Long Island iced tea?"

Big Mac's eyes widened in sudden understanding. "Yes...yes. I didn't even notice. I was making so many drinks at the time."

Raina's heart sank. She should have known. When she had spoken with Leilani in her apartment, that person seemed to have forgotten their friendship. And at the bar, Leilani seemed to have forgotten about her favorite cocktail drink. "That wasn't Leilani. That was Ailani pretending to be her sister."

14

MISTAKEN IDENTITY

Raina pulled a ten-dollar bill from her purse and tossed it on the bar table. She strode to the entrance of the bar and paused to look back over her shoulder. Big Mac clutched the Leilani cocktail in his hands, staring at it as if the answers would bubble forth like it was one of those Magic 8 Ball toys. He appeared equally as stunned at the discovery that the wrong twin was identified as the victim.

She trotted out of the bar and into the restaurant. She burst into the kitchen, calling out, "Leilani! Where are you?"

A cook came over, clutching a metal ladle in front of him like it was a weapon. "You can't be back here."

"It's okay," Raina said, holding out her hands, palms out. "I'm Leilani's cousin. Auntie May is my great-aunt."

The cook gave Raina the stink eye. "I don't care who you are, young lady. Get out of my kitchen."

Raina took one last glance around. Unless her cousin was in the walk-in freezer, she wasn't in the kitchen. "Sorry." She backed out of the kitchen, just in case the cook decided to toss the ladle at the back of her head. She scanned the dining area. No Leilani.

Outside in the lobby, Raina called Leilani's cell phone. It rang several times and went to voicemail. She dialed the numbers again. This time, someone picked up the phone.

"Hello, Rainy?" Po Po said.

Raina swallowed the lump in her throat. Her grandma had just confirmed her suspicion that her cousin was dead. "Po Po, where are you? How did you get this phone?"

"I am still inside the office with Auntie May. A phone started ringing, and I found it in the Lost and Found box," Po Po said. "Your name came up on the display, so I picked up the call."

"How did the phone get inside the Lost and Found box?" Raina asked.

Po Po turned away from the phone to speak to Auntie May. Raina couldn't hear their muffled conversation.

When Po Po came back on the line, she said, "The landscaper found it this morning in a potted plant in the walkway from the pool to the outdoor dining patio. Who are you trying to call?"

Raina opened her mouth, but no words came out. Did the killer knock her cousin out on the pathway and drag her body to the underground oven? She glanced at the one-way window of her great-aunt's office, knowing her grandma was probably looking out. Her vision blurred at the sudden tears. "Give... give me a minute," she finally managed to squeeze out in a shaky voice. She tapped on the screen to end the call.

She stumbled her way to the public restroom between the convenience store and the concierge desk. Once inside a stall, she locked the door and sat on the toilet to cry. For the first time, she would fail her family. Things would not return to normal.

Even if Raina solved Leilani's murder, the Hawaiian branch of the family would fall apart. Raina didn't wish for Ailani to die in her sister's place, but she wasn't the responsible one—living at home and helping out her grandma. Ailani didn't leave behind big shoes to fill.

There was a knock on the stall door. "Rainy, is that you?" Po Po called out.

Raina pulled out some toilet paper, wiped her face, and blew her nose. She took a deep breath and opened the door.

Po Po's eyes were filled with concern. "Is it Matthew? Did something happen to him?"

Raina shook her head. "I was calling Leilani, and you picked up the phone."

"When did Leilani lose her phone? And how come she didn't know it was missing by now?" Po Po said.

"My cousin didn't lose her phone." Raina told her grandma why she believed Ailani was pretending to be her sister.

When Po Po made the connection, her eyes filled with tears. "Leilani is dead, isn't she?" Her voice was thick with emotion.

Raina nodded, brushing away another tear. "I wish it weren't so."

Po Po pulled Raina into a bear hug. For such a tiny woman, her grandma could squeeze pretty hard. Po Po patted the back of Raina's head. Probably relieved that her granddaughter was alive and guilty for feeling this way.

"May will be devastated when she hears the news," Po Po said.

"We need to contact Detective Mars about my suspicion. The police will probably use dental records to confirm which twin is the victim."

Raina went to the sink and washed her face with a wet paper towel. While crying was a good outlet for her pent-up emotions, it had never gotten her anywhere in the past. As far as she was concerned, action was the most effective way to combat grief.

Po Po cleaned her face at the other sink. She met Raina's eyes in the mirror. "Why is Ailani pretending to be Leilani?"

"That's the million-dollar question we need to find

out. I hope Ailani doesn't have anything to do with her sister's death."

"What do we do next?" Po Po asked.

"I want to confront Ailani, but it's better if we do nothing until we have more information."

"What about the landscaper who found the phone?"

"With the rain, I'm not sure we'll find anything, but we should look at the pathway. To check every box. And we have to get in touch with Detective Mars later." Raina's mouth twisted into a grimace. "I'm not looking forward to the conversation."

"Do we tell May about Leilani?" Po Po asked.

Raina hesitated. The police still needed to confirm the identity of the victim. She shook her head reluctantly. "The news has to come from the police. We don't know what Ailani is up to yet, but I don't want to scare her off. We should hold on to Leilani's cell phone though. I don't want someone claiming it by accident."

Po Po patted her beach bag tote. "I pocketed it when May wasn't looking. Now let's rock and roll."

The two of them returned to the office and got Auntie May to radio the head landscaper who found the cell phone. Luckily, Auntie May was more concerned about payroll than questioning why they needed to talk to her staff. The landscaper said he would meet them poolside in about an hour after he finished his work.

Raina and Po Po grabbed prepackaged sandwiches

from the convenience store for a late lunch. They went upstairs to Po Po's hotel room. The room held a full-size bed, a desk, and a chest of drawers with an old box TV on top. The beachfront view from the balcony made up for the Spartan room. The door connecting the two adjacent rooms was wide open.

After Raina checked on Win in the adjacent room—he was fast asleep—she filled her grandma in on her conversation with the fake Leilani and Big Mac.

"How many things do we have going on here?" Po Po said. She held up her hand and ticked the points off her finger. "Leilani is dead, and Ailani is pretending to be her sister. Ailani is the bookkeeper for an illegal gambling ring. Sonny Kwan is looking for Ailani because he wants to take down this illegal gambling ring. But doesn't it belong to his criminal organization?"

Raina nodded. "Sonny probably doesn't know all the day-to-day details, so he doesn't have access to the offshore account numbers or the names of everyone that might be involved. And you need this information to pull it up by the roots."

"Wouldn't somebody in the Nine Dragons eventually become suspicious about Sonny's loyalty? Every time he shows up, a local branch of the business gets shut down by the FBI."

Raina chewed her lower lip. She wasn't sure how much to share with Po Po, but her grandma was completely trustworthy. "I think that's why the feds are teaming Matthew up with Sonny. If things go south, they are just two buddies meeting up for coffee. Sometimes when Matthew disappears for weeks at a time without even a phone call at night, I don't sleep the entire time he's gone. He promises to stop taking these risks once we have a family."

"Matthew's been to Afghanistan and a few other dangerous parts of the world. He knows how to take care of himself."

Raina shook her head. "This is different. It's espionage and going undercover. What if it catches up to us in his normal life?"

"Then you go and take on a new identity until it is safe to come home."

Raina gaped at Po Po. What did her grandma know about creating secret identities? "You make it sound so simple."

"When you have money and connections, it is simple."

"We don't have either one of those."

Po Po patted Raina's hand. "I do."

Raina didn't know if her grandma was exaggerating like she did when chatting with the senior citizens at home, but she got a Taser and her stink bombs to Hawaii. This meant she must have something extra up her sleeve. "Back to the investigation. Ailani practically pointed her finger at Detective Mars. He might be part of this illegal gambling ring."

"Do you think Leilani was mistaken for Ailani?" Po

Po asked. "And she was killed to prevent her from handing over the account numbers and names to the feds?"

Raina thought back to her conversation with Ailani and shook her head reluctantly. "Ailani told me that she wasn't a snitch, and she needed the ransom money to get away from the organization. So, I don't think she is working with the feds."

Po Po frowned. "I'm lost. If Leilani's death has nothing to do with the Nine Dragons, why would someone kill her? Like you said, this wasn't an accidental or random death. You have to do some serious planning to know the staff schedule and get the body inside the imu."

"What if the killer had meant to kill Leilani, and Ailani assuming her sister's identity was just an opportunist taking advantage of the situation?"

"Okay. Go on," Po Po said, sounding doubtful. "Leilani was a pillar of the community."

"But this didn't mean she hadn't made a mistake in the past. She was involved in the car accident that killed Sarah Harris in high school. I wonder if Ailani was the other girl in the car and which one of the twins was the driver that night."

"That was a long time ago."

"And yet, Jenny Harris is in town to visit her sister's grave."

Po Po gasped, clapping her hands over her mouth. "No. Jenny can't be the killer. She's too sweet."

"Why are you talking about Jenny?" Win called out from the adjoining hotel room. He appeared in the doorway, his hair loose around his shoulders. He strode into Po Po's room and picked through the remains of their sandwiches.

If Raina didn't let him in on what she had found out, he might get himself into a dangerous situation, especially if Jenny Harris turned out to be Leilani's killer. Raina filled him in. When she was done, he appeared dazed.

Win rolled the turkey slice around his finger. "Why do you think Jenny is the killer?"

"I think the car accident was the catalyst that made her family fall apart. Afterward, her parents divorced." Raina paused, trying to recall the details of her conversation with Jenny in the ER waiting room. "I wonder if her parents remarried. If both her parents were able to move on, Jenny might even feel that her parents betrayed her sister somehow."

"It doesn't make any sense," Win said defensively. "I was about the same age when Dad died, and I didn't turn into a psycho killer."

Raina gave her grandma a pointed look. Her brother was in denial. She wondered if he would have reacted differently if he didn't have feelings for Jenny.

She returned her attention to her brother. "First, Dad died from a disease. There is no one to blame. Second, you weren't neglected. Mom knew she couldn't take care of us and moved the family back in with our grandparents. And with all the uncles and aunts popping in at Po Po's house, we probably had a lot more attention than when Dad was alive."

Win crossed his arms and shook his head. "Jenny was with me all day. We hung out with several people by the rental shack. I'm not her only alibi."

Raina groaned inwardly. She didn't want to argue with her brother. Even if they had spent all afternoon together, he wasn't with Jenny every minute. It was simple enough to claim a stomachache and disappear for fifteen or twenty minutes to knock the victim out. But how did she hide the body until she had time to move it to the underground oven?

"I didn't say Jenny is the killer," Raina said in what she hoped was a soothing tone. "I just said she could be the killer. So, she's on our suspect list. Please be careful when you're spending time with her."

"And don't mention any of this or the investigation to Jenny," Po Po said. "Until she's eliminated from the suspect list, we have to be careful."

Win glared first at Raina and then at Po Po. "Fine, but the two of you are wrong. And I am going to prove it."

Raina didn't like his mulish tone. He was digging in his heels, and this could compromise the investigation. "How are you feeling? I thought you're not supposed to sleep when you have a concussion."

Win shrugged. "I feel fine. Who else is on your

suspect list?" His tone implied that Jenny better not be their only suspect.

"What about Big Mac?" Po Po said.

"How is he related to all this?" Win asked.

"He was Sarah's boyfriend at the time of her death," Raina said.

Win smacked the table with his palm. "He's the killer."

"Big Mac claims he was in love with Leilani," Raina said. "He even invented a drink for her."

"Maybe it's a front," Win said. "To hide his tracks."

"That seems to be a long shot," Po Po said. "Even if Big Mac still suffered somehow over Sarah's death, he had waited a really long time to get his revenge on Leilani. They have been working together since high school. He had plenty of opportunities to kill her. Why didn't he do it before now?"

"What if Jenny's visit was the catalyst?" Raina said slowly. "Maybe she had information that changed everything for him."

"We have gone to the bar to grab drinks a few times," Win said. "But I don't remember the two of them chatting. They don't appear to recognize each other. Besides, Jenny was a child back then. Big Mac probably has no recollection of her."

Raina turned to her grandma. "Auntie May will probably give us access to the hotel cameras, but I don't want to sit through days of video looking for something suspicious. Maybe your hacker friend has software to process the video and look for Jenny, Big Mac, and Leilani." She frowned. Who hadn't they talked to yet? "The blond bartender that gave Leilani the second drink." She described the man—his height, the glasses, and the mole on the side of his chin.

"I don't remember anyone with a mole on his chin walking around the resort," Win said.

"Maybe it's a fake mole like a sticker," Po Po said.

Raina nodded. "Big Mac doesn't recall seeing this person at the bar either. Of course, he could be lying. But the hotel videos might have recorded the blond bartender."

Po Po gave Raina a salute. "I'm on it, Sherlock. I'll tell my hacker to keep an eye out for Mr. Moley Mole."

"Who is Mr. Moley Mole?" Win asked.

Po Po pointed to the side of her chin. "The blond man with the mole."

Raina shook her head. Whatever floated her grandma's boat. If given half the chance, Po Po would refer to everyone by their code names. "By the way, did your friend find out anything from Ailani's cell phone records?"

"It finally all makes sense now," Po Po said. She pulled her tablet out and tapped on the screen to show the dots on a map. "Using the cell signals, my hacker tracked Ailani's cell phones to these locations after her death. We thought maybe someone stole the phone or found it. But now we know it's actually Ailani using her phone."

Raina stared at the spots on the map. Most of them were concentrated around the resort. "This pretty much confirms that Ailani is pretending to be her sister. What a mess." She glanced at her smartwatch. "It's time to meet the landscaper. Win, you're coming with us. We might need your muscles."

Now that Jenny was at the top of the suspect list, Raina would have to keep Win by her side for the rest of the trip. Of course, Win would never do anything intentionally to jeopardize Raina or Po Po's safety, but he might let something slip. Or Win might take it upon himself to do some surveillance on Jenny and get caught. And with the imminent heartbreak coming on the horizon, it might be best that he spent more time with the family.

15

A TRESPASSER

The head landscaper was a wiry old Japanese man about Po Po's age. He was an inch taller than Raina and wore a yellow raincoat and boots. Japanese people were generally one of the more polite cultures, but the head landscaper was a bit of a grouch. Once he confirmed their identity, he turned and strode away without further words.

Po Po followed his lead, and Raina and Win hurried after their grandma. As the head landscaper led the way to a large kukui tree in the man-made grove between the pool and luau dining area, he mumbled unhappily underneath his breath. He pointed at the tree and left.

"Now what?" Win asked, holding his jacket over his head. "My toes are getting cold."

Raina glanced at her younger brother's feet. He had

on flip-flop sandals. "We should look around the area and see if there are any clues."

"What are we looking for?" Po Po asked.

Raina shrugged. "Anything that looks out of place. Maybe a flattened area that indicates this was where the murderer killed or hid Leilani's body. I don't know. Just keep your eyes open."

"The rain probably washed everything away by now," Win complained.

"Just look around," Raina said.

For the next few minutes, the three of them each slowly walked in a different direction, keeping their eyes on the ground. Raina circled back to the kukui tree. Even their footprints had disappeared in the short time they were looking elsewhere. Maybe her brother was right. This was a wasted effort.

"Rainy! Does broken glass count?" Win called out.

Raina and Po Po trotted over to Win. He pointed at the broken glass and the smashed cocktail paper umbrella on the dirt. The three of them bent down for a closer look.

"What are we looking at?" Po Po asked. "Someone's cocktail drink?"

"Yes," Win said. "Could be from any of the guests. You can't tell how long it's been out here."

"It's pretty recent," Raina said. "The red color on the paper umbrella is still bright. If it had been here for a while, the sun would have faded the color by now. I wonder if it's Leilani's cocktail from the day she disappeared." Raina explained how her cousin had wandered around the bar, talking into her cell phone and sipping her second drink. "Maybe she was heading toward the outdoor dining patio."

"Sounds good enough to get it checked out," Po Po said. She pulled out plastic gloves and a Ziploc bag from her beach bag tote and handed it to Win. "Bag it up, Inspector Lestrade."

Win put on the gloves. "Who is Inspector Lestrade?"

"He's the police in the Sherlock Holmes stories."

"I like the code name." Win reached for the broken glass.

Raina stopped her brother. "What are you doing? We shouldn't take things from the crime scene."

"First, if the police cared, they would have found this themselves," Po Po said. "Second, if we don't bag it, it might get washed away. The rain isn't stopping anytime soon."

"You have a point," Raina said. "Do we hand it over to Detective Mars?"

Po Po shrugged. "It's your call, Sherlock. But if we touch this, it's probably no longer permissible in court."

Raina chewed her lower lip. "Win, go into the kitchen of the restaurant and ask for a big mixing bowl. We can put it over the broken glass."

"Isn't this still contaminating the crime scene?" Win said.

"Yes, but that's still better than removing it," Raina said.

Win jogged in the direction of the restaurant.

"If Detective Mars wants nothing to do with this, we can come back to collect it later," Po Po said.

"What can we do with it?" Raina said. "It's not like we can get a lab to analyze it to see if the drink was drugged."

"Why not?" Po Po asked.

Raina stared at her grandma. "There's a private lab on the island?"

"Not a private lab, but I can get a teenager from the nearby high school to analyze it. I'll have to pay the expedited fee." Po Po shrugged. "But it can be done."

Raina gaped at Po Po. Her grandma, the internet, and social media were a scary combination.

Win returned with a big metal mixing bowl. Raina put it upside down over the broken glass and put a large rock on top of it.

"What's the rock for?" Win asked.

"To hold it down," Raina said. "I'm afraid the wind might pick up and blow everything away."

"Time to change into dry clothes," Po Po said.

"And put on something more waterproof," Raina said. "Then we're off to Ailani's apartment. Win, you're the driver. Po Po, you're the navigator. I'll call Detective Mars from the backseat. If he doesn't want the broken glass, then Po Po can send it to the high schooler to get it analyzed."

Not for the first time, Raina was glad that her grandma was willing to foot the bill for their sleuthing. While Raina might not have much money of her own, having generous relatives who did was just as good.

Win wiped the water dripping off the end of his nose. "Do we have to go now? Some of the local streets might be flooded."

Raina would love nothing more than to curl up in her suite with a book and a box of chocolates. But she had a feeling—almost a compulsion—to keep digging while the trail was blazing hot. And Raina didn't want Sonny Kwan to get to Ailani's apartment before she did.

"Then I suggest you change quickly," Raina said, "and figure out how to get around the flooding. Maybe watch the traffic news or something."

Win groaned. "I'm still hungry. I only had the leftover residue from your sandwiches."

"Quit your yapping, Inspector Lestrade, or next time we won't include you in the fun," Po Po said. "We can grab another sandwich on the way to our rooms."

"Two sandwiches and a coconut water," Win said.

"Deal." Po Po held out her hand. "Let's synchronize our watches."

WIN PULLED the minivan slowly out of the staff parking lot. The windshield wipers were at full speed but couldn't keep up with the downpour. It was hard to see beyond a few yards in front of them. Maybe it was a bad idea to drive around the unfamiliar narrow roads, but the big storm was supposed to hit tomorrow. Their window of opportunity for driving around the island was closing.

In the passenger seat, Po Po tapped on her tablet. Raina wondered what kind of cell service her grandma had to get a reliable signal in this weather. "Okay, I sent the hotel videos to my hacker to process. He has photos of Jenny, the twins, and Big Mac, so he knows who he's searching for."

In the backseat, Raina dialed Detective Mars's cell phone number. It rang several times and went to voicemail. Since Ailani wanted the detective investigated, Raina assumed she couldn't trust this shady cop. She hung up. It was a bad idea to withhold information from the police, but she didn't want the detective to know that Ailani was still alive. If only Matthew were here with them. He would know who they could trust.

The ten-minute drive to her cousin's apartment took forty minutes. There weren't many cars on the road, but everyone, including them, was traveling at snail speed. For some crazy reason, Raina had always assumed Hawaii was sunny year-round. Was this the Pineapple Express everyone kept mentioning?

The parking lot for Ailani's apartment complex was flooded with several inches of rain, but the street in front of the complex was clear. Someone probably hadn't removed the debris covering up the storm drain. If the water rose another three inches, it would flood the units on the first floor.

Raina wondered why someone didn't clean out the storm drain or put sandbags in front of the first-floor units to hold back the water. She knew this was her engineering background commenting in her head. Sometimes she wondered if she should go back to that career. It certainly would triple her meager salary working at the senior center. But then, she wouldn't get to spend as much time with her grandma, and that wasn't something money could buy.

Win drove past the apartment and parked on the curb a block away. Raina, Po Po, and Win pulled up the hoods of their thin disposable ponchos—courtesy of the convenience store at the resort—before leaving the warmth of the minivan. Raina led the way back to the apartment complex.

As soon as Raina stepped into the water flooding the parking lot, her toes protested at the cold. There were no rubber boots at the convenience store, and Raina and Win still wore their sandals. Her grandma had somehow fit her orthopedic rubber boots and her other paraphernalia into her small red suitcase.

The crusty green paint peeled away from the apartment building's exterior walls, and several outdoor lights were missing bulbs. Raina was right about the storm drain. Several inches of muck and leaves blocked the metal grate. Win could have removed the debris with a shovel in less than ten minutes. Since no one bothered with the storm drain, this spoke volumes about the people who lived here.

They found Ailani's unit quickly, and Raina unlocked the door for them. As she stepped inside, she heard the sound of something hitting the floor. Was someone inside? Did this person knock over something? She held out her hand to stop her grandma and brother from charging inside.

"Is someone here? I'm Raina, Ailani's cousin," Raina called out, even though she knew her cousin wasn't actually in the apartment. Ailani had given Raina the key, knowing full well that Raina would search the place. If Ailani had wanted to remove personal items or evidence, she would have done so before giving Raina the key. No, the person inside the apartment was definitely a foe. Was this someone from the Nine Dragons Triad? Or Leilani's killer?

Raina strained her ears but didn't hear the sound again.

"What is it, Sis?" Win whispered.

"I thought I heard someone inside," Raina whispered back.

Po Po pulled out a handful of stink bombs. "Let's smoke them out."

Raina's gaze shifted to her grandma. "No—"

Po Po tossed the stink bombs into the apartment.

Ping! Ping! Ping!

The tiny glass vials exploded against the linoleum

floor, releasing skunk funk and rotten kimchi into the air.

Even before Raina was fully aware of what happened, her body reacted by gagging.

Po Po grabbed Raina's arm and pulled her out of the apartment.

Win slammed the front door shut and ran around the building. "I'll watch the back in case someone climbs out a window," he called out over his shoulder.

Raina bent over and spat out the bile in her throat. It didn't matter how many times she smelled her grandma's stink bombs. She would never get used to it. Po Po stood next to Raina, rubbing her back. Either her grandma was used to the smell, or she didn't have any more senses left in her nostrils.

The front door opened, and Detective Mars stumbled out, coughing and choking.

Po Po reached behind him and slammed the door shut. She stood in front of him, daring him to push her out of the way.

"Detective Mars," Raina said, straightening. She swallowed, ignoring the unpleasant taste in her mouth. "What are you doing here?"

Detective Mars wiped at the snot dripping out of his nose with his hand and rubbed it on the thighs of his jeans, leaving a wet trail.

Po Po openly smirked and handed him a packet of tissues. "Are you trespassing on private property?"

Detective Mars blew his nose, but it still kept dripping. He straightened to his full height and squared his shoulders as if this would give him more authority. "I have permission to be here." He pulled a key from his hip pocket. "Before Ailani's death, she gave me a key."

Raina raised an eyebrow. Did Ailani hand out the key to her apartment like it was Halloween candy? "Were the two of you in a relationship?"

Detective Mars nodded. "We were close...friends."

"Were you friends with benefits?" Po Po asked, winking.

Detective Mars's red, irritated eyes glared at Po Po. "No. Get your mind out of the gutter, lady."

Raina shot her grandma a stern look. She didn't want this conversation to get derailed. This was the perfect opportunity to tell the police what she had found out about the identity of the victim. But she just didn't trust the detective. Why wasn't he upset that his "close friend" had died? "You didn't answer my question. What are you doing here? Are you searching for something?" As soon as the words left her mouth, Raina knew she was onto something.

"I don't have to answer you," Detective Mars said, holding out an arm like he intended to push Raina aside.

Po Po whipped out her pepper spray, aiming at his face. "Go ahead. Make my day, buddy."

Detective Mars took a step back and bumped his elbow into the front door, glaring at them. "Do I have to charge you for obstructing an investigation?"

"Ailani is my cousin, and her apartment isn't a crime scene," Raina said. "And you need permission from the family or a warrant to search the premises." She blinked at him innocently. "I don't think we're the ones breaking the law."

Detective Mars narrowed his eyes. "A Smart Alec like your husband. Just because he came from a big city, he thought he could throw his weight around." He glanced around the parking lot. "I am surprised he's not here with you."

Raina bristled at the comment. It sounded like Detective Mars might be jealous of her husband's expertise. She wasn't offended about being called a Smart Alec, but she was mighty particular when other people made remarks about her wonderful husband. She took a deep breath. But there was no point in antagonizing the local law enforcement. And he had to be hiding something if he wasn't even upset at the stink bombs.

"Isn't it a conflict of interest for you to investigate the case?" Raina asked. She was getting him to squeal one way or another.

"What conflict?" Detective Mars said.

"You're my cousin's boyfriend."

"We only dated a few times, and that was a long time ago," Detective Mars said.

Raina raised an eyebrow. Which cousin was he talking about? Detective Mars dated Leilani a long time ago while Ailani was his more recent girlfriend.

Was he searching Ailani's apartment for the backups of the names and account numbers for the gambling ring? "This still doesn't give you permission to be in my cousin's apartment."

"I am here to pick something up," Detective Mars said.

Raina made a big show at glancing at his hands and his jeans pockets. "What did you pick up?"

"My phone," he said tersely.

"When we discovered Ailani's body at the luau, you had your phone then," Raina said. "What is it doing in her apartment after her death?"

Detective Mars blinked as if trying to come up with a lie. Maybe he assumed she would overlook small details. "I don't have to put up with this."

Raina pulled out her cell phone and dialed nine-one-one. She held it up for Detective Mars to see. Her finger hovered over the green button to make the call. "Either I see what's in your pockets, or we can call the police, and an officer can go through your pockets. And then we can charge you for trespassing. And we will file a complaint with your department about your conflict of interest in my cousin's death. Trust me—my grandma can make a big stink about this."

Detective Mars narrowed his eyes. "Are you threatening me?"

Raina swallowed. A small part of her was afraid, but she was even more fearful that he would leave with evidence that could take down the illegal gambling ring. It might be a small link in a long chain that could unravel the whole Nine Dragons organization. Since Matthew was working with Sonny Kwan, Raina wasn't going to let evidence disappear on her watch.

Win came back from behind the building. "Nobody is out back." He paused, his eyes shifting between his grandma and the detective. He jogged over and flanked his grandma. He didn't say a word, but suddenly the air changed.

Maybe it was the messy man bun. Or the scruff on his face. But there was something feral about her younger brother. A sort of wild energy. Whatever it was, it made Detective Mars hesitate.

As Detective Mars's gaze shifted between Raina and Win, he licked his lower lip nervously. "Are you guys crazy? You can't do this. I'm the police."

Po Po waved the pepper spray in front of his face again. "I am old and senile. I'll get off with nothing more than a hand slap."

Win crossed his arms, showing off his biceps. "And I'm barely an adult. Too young to know any better. I'll get off with a hand slap, too."

Raina suppressed the urge to roll her eyes. "Turn out your pockets. I want to make sure you didn't take anything from here."

Detective Mars did as he was told—pulling out his cell phone, wallet, and a set of keys. "Satisfied?" He snarled.

Raina took the key ring. On it was a panda head

charm that looked too cute for a grown man to carry around. She removed it from the ring.

"Hey, that's mine," Detective Mars said.

"It belongs to my cousin. I have seen it on her key ring," Raina lied. The panda charm might be a mini-USB storage stick. She also removed the key to Ailani's apartment and tossed the key ring back to the detective.

Detective Mars's hands curled into fists. "Give me back my charm."

"If Leilani says you can have it, then I'll give it back to you," Raina said. "But this belongs to my family."

Detective Mars pointed his fingers at Raina like he was aiming a gun at her. "You're a dead woman."

16

PINEAPPLE EXPRESS

They did a cursory search of Ailani's one-bedroom apartment but didn't find anything to help with the investigation.

"Do we still need to worry about clearing out the apartment?" Po Po asked.

Raina shook her head. "The truth will come out eventually, and Ailani probably still wants her stuff. She can't slip into Leilani's life forever."

They returned to the minivan, and Win made slow progress back to the resort. The rain was falling so hard now that they couldn't see more than a few feet in front of them. They could probably walk faster back to the resort, except the rain and cold would make it a miserable experience.

Raina pulled the panda head charm out of her pocket and turned on the minivan's dome light. It was about the size of the first joint on her pinky finger. The plastic was smooth all around. If this was a USB storage stick, Raina didn't know how to open it. There was nothing on the charm that indicated it was an electronic device. However, if Detective Mars wanted it so badly that he was willing to threaten Raina with death, it must be important.

She shivered at his threat. Was she walking around with a big target on her back? If nothing else, Detective Mars had just confirmed that he was part of the islands' illegal gambling ring. She didn't know if he was high up on the hierarchy or a low-level goon.

But if he was willing to threaten Raina publicly, this meant he had no fear of her filing a complaint with his supervisors at his legitimate day job. Maybe the corruption went all the way to the top of the police force. No, there had to be a good cop in the department. She refused to believe that every single one of them was crooked.

Raina couldn't figure out why Ailani didn't keep the panda charm with her. Or why she didn't have a better hiding spot for it than the apartment. And how was it that Detective Mars was able to find it so easily? The backup was supposed to be Ailani's insurance so that the Nine Dragons couldn't make her disappear into the ocean.

Po Po turned around in the passenger seat. "Rainy, why did you take the panda charm?" she said, raising her voice. The battering rain on the minivan was loud as a drum.

"I thought maybe it was a memory stick, but I can't seem to find an opening where you would plug it into a computer," Raina said.

Po Po held out her palm. "Let me take a look at it." Her grandma studied the charm. "It's a solid piece. You'll need a screwdriver to pry it open. I don't think it is supposed to work like that, though."

She pulled out her tablet and tapped on the screen. "Hot diggity dog. I can connect to the panda charm through Bluetooth. I wonder if that's how you transfer the data." She tapped on the screen again and frowned. "Oh no, it needs a password code."

"Can your hacker friend get into it?" Win asked, his eyes on the road.

"We will have to mail it to him," Po Po mumbled, still tapping on the screen, probably trying to input various passcode combinations.

Raina shook her head. "We should turn it over to Matthew. If it contains sensitive information about the Nine Dragons triad, I don't want your hacker to get on their hit list."

"Good thinking," Po Po said.

Lightning flashed across the sky and rumbled thunderously. It was pitch black outside. Raina was too focused on the panda charm before, but she finally noticed that the minivan seemed to shake from the wind. For the first time, Raina was nervous about the weather.

"Are we almost back at the resort?" Raina asked.

"The last mile," Win said. He had a death grip on the steering wheel.

The last mile was the most treacherous—a mountain wall looming on one side and a deep drop to a ravine on the other. Raina settled back into her seat, clutching the armrest and praying to their ancestors. Even Po Po grew quiet so that Win could focus on the road. Time seemed to slow to a crawl. The storm that was supposed to come in during the wee hours of the night was probably on top of them now.

Raina's thoughts wandered to her husband. She hoped he had the sense to stay on the ground. And she probably wouldn't see him for the next few days. It would take some time to get flights back in the air again. She missed his comforting presence.

The three of them made it back to the resort after eight p.m. Heavy rain pounded on their thin ponchos as they power walked from the staff parking lot to the lobby. They trudged over to the Wayfarer restaurant, leaving a trail of wet puddles on the tile floor. The lights were off, and the sign on the door said the restaurant was closed for the night.

"I bet they couldn't fix the walk-in freezer this time," Po Po said.

Win's stomach rumbled, and he rubbed it. "Let's hope they still have those prepackaged sandwiches at the convenience store."

Raina had a sinking feeling in the pit of her stomach. At this hour, and with the horrible weather, most sensible people would stay put at the resort. Unfortunately, this meant they probably went to the convenience store to scrounge for food.

They traipsed across the lobby again, leaving another trail of wet puddles to the convenience store. Sure enough, there were no prepackaged sandwiches. Instead, on the shelves were five instant noodle cups, one dark chocolate bar, and a bag of macadamia nuts.

Win grabbed all the instant noodle cups. "A feast."

Po Po got everything from the shelves. "Rainy, look in the refrigerator. Grab whatever you can."

Raina strode over to the refrigerator. There were six bottles of water and four cans of Hawaiian Sun juice drinks. She turned away from the fridge to ask, "How many drinks do you want?"

A man reached into the refrigerator, took all four cans of the juice drinks, and strolled over to the cashier.

"Hey, I was planning to buy those cans," Raina called out.

"You snooze, you lose," the man said, paying for his purchase. He strolled out of the convenience store and gave Raina a backward wave.

In another aisle, Win held a bag over his head. "I found some Doritos!"

After paying for their haul, the three of them went upstairs to Po Po's room. Win disappeared into the adjoining room to change, locking the door behind him.

"Are you returning to your suite tonight?" Po Po asked.

Raina shook her head. "I don't want to walk back in this storm. It looks like we're roommates for the night."

Po Po offered Raina red-and-white striped pajamas. "Go shower first and get out of the wet clothes. You're a lot wetter than I am."

Raina glanced at the pajamas. Great. She got to be a peppermint stick for the night. She went into the bathroom, showered, and changed. She opened the bathroom door to find both Po Po and Win slurping the instant noodle cups and watching the news.

Po Po pointed at the coffee maker. "There's still hot water in there." She gulped the soup and went into the bathroom.

The evening passed uneventfully. Between the three of them, they ate everything they bought from the convenience store. Win even went to bed slightly hungry. Everyone hoped the restaurant would be open for business the following day.

Raina tossed and turned for several hours and finally drifted off in an uneasy slumber at one in the morning. Who knew a storm sounded so loud?

Bam! Bam!

Raina drifted back to consciousness. She glanced around the dim room. From the illumination coming off all the devices charging at the desk, she could make out Po Po next to her on the bed, rolled up in the comforter like a hot dog. The adjoining door was still open, and Raina could make out the dark lump of her brother on the bed.

Raina glanced at her smartwatch. Two in the morning. She had barely slept an hour. She yawned, feeling the pull of sleep. Maybe she was hearing things. She snuggled back in bed, pulling the covers over her ears.

Bam! Bam!

Raina sat up again and glanced at the door that opened to the hallway. She definitely heard something this time.

"Hey, Po Po. Raina Sun's grandma! Open the door."

Raina's eyes widened. What was Sonny Kwan doing at the resort in the middle of the night? And how did he know this was her grandma's room?

Next to Raina, Po Po stirred in her sleep. She pushed the eye mask up to her forehead. "Did someone call me?" She yawned so widely that Raina could see her molars.

The door handle rattled like someone was trying to get into the room.

Po Po pulled her pepper spray out from under her pillow. "Win, wake up. Someone is breaking into my room."

Win rolled and fell off the bed. He cursed.

Raina looked through the peephole. Yep, it was Sonny Kwan. The door across from Po Po's room was opened, and the man in pajamas told Sonny to shut his trap. Either Po Po's neighbor was too sleepy to notice the scar on Sonny's face, or he was too stupid to care.

Even at this late hour, Sonny looked every bit like trouble in designer jeans.

A door clicked open, and Win came into view in the peephole. "It's the middle of the night, buddy. If you can't find your room, go down to the front desk."

As far as Raina knew, Sonny Kwan had never seen Win. It was even harder to see any similarity between Raina and her younger brother with the man bun and scruffy face. However, Raina couldn't understand why her brother felt the need to stick his nose out in the hallway. He should have kept his room door locked.

"I am looking for a little old Chinese lady," Sonny said. He held out his hand to his armpit. "She's about this tall. White hair. Lots of energy like she's high on something."

"Back for more already, huh?" Po Po called out. She waved the pepper spray in the air. "Didn't you get enough of me this morning?"

Raina did a double take at the peephole. She groaned out loud. Her grandma was standing out there next to Win in her gray silk pajamas. What was wrong with her family? Didn't they know not to open the door to gangsters in the middle of the night? Weren't they taught at a young age that strangers meant danger?

Sonny took a step toward Po Po. "So, it was you in the chicken costume. I knew it. You're a crazy old bird."

Raina better get a handle on the situation, or no one would get any sleep tonight. She unlocked Po Po's door.

"Come on in, Sonny," Raina said.

The neighbor looked Raina up and down. "The next time you get freaky with a gigolo, keep it down. The rest of us are trying to sleep." He shut the door before Raina could say anything.

Win and Po Po burst out laughing.

Raina couldn't believe she had to deal with the peanut gallery at this hour tonight. She shifted her gaze to Sonny, who was grinning from ear to ear. He appeared to enjoy her embarrassment. As long as he was happy, he wouldn't think about killing her grandma.

Win and Po Po disappeared back into Win's room. The two of them appeared in the adjoining doorway. Win folded his arms across his chest, his gaze scanning up and down Sonny's body. Whatever he saw put him on high alert, because his eyes followed the triad leader like he expected trouble.

Sonny strolled into the room and sat down on the swivel chair by the desk. He flicked on the desk lamp. "What did you do, Rainy, for someone in my organization to put a price on your head?"

17

A LATE NIGHT GUEST

Raina gaped at him, her mouth drying up with fear. She sank onto the edge of the bed.

"Did you say someone wants to kill my sister?" Win asked.

Po Po narrowed her eyes, and her fingers tightened around the pepper spray. "I bet you it's that low-down dog Timothy Mars."

It had only been a few hours since Raina removed the panda head charm from the detective's key ring. She hadn't really taken his threat seriously. After all, she had been involved in enough murder investigations where one or more of the suspects threatened her with bodily harm.

But you're playing with the big boys, and they kill for fun, said a small voice inside her head. Raina shivered.

"Are you here to warn me or to kill me?" Raina

asked. She was proud that her voice did not quiver even though her insides felt like Jell-O.

"I came here to save you, my lovely, but I was too late," Sonny said.

Riiing! Riiing!

Raina jumped and shifted her gaze to Po Po's cell phone plugged in at the side table next to the bed. It rang again. Auntie May's name appeared on the screen. A phone call in the middle of the night was always bad news. Could it be any worse than having a triad leader in their room?

Po Po crossed the room and picked up the phone. "Hello?" She listened for a long moment. "She's safe." She hung up and turned a steely gaze at Sonny. "Young man, you have some explaining to do."

Sonny ignored Po Po and focused his attention on Raina. "Can we talk in private?"

Raina nodded. She turned to her grandma and said, "Why don't you go hang out in Win's room for a bit?"

Po Po stared at Raina like she was crazy. She leaned forward and whispered, "You shouldn't be alone with the big, bad Wolf."

Raina flicked a glance at Sonny. He grinned back at her, showing his teeth. She was crazy for agreeing to be alone with him. While there was a price on her head, she must have faith that they were temporary allies. Besides, he probably wanted her grandma out of the way. It was too late in the night to deal with her grand-ma's antics.

"We'll close the door, but we won't lock it," Raina said.

After a few more minutes of grumbling, Raina finally got her grandma and brother out of the room. She had a feeling the two of them would have their ears glued to the adjoining door. If she were in their place, she would do the same thing.

Raina returned to the bed and faced Sonny. "What do you mean by too late?"

Sonny leaned forward and lowered his voice. "That phone call was probably the bad news. Someone blew up the honeymoon suite."

If Raina weren't sitting down, her legs would have collapsed from underneath her. If it weren't for the storm, she would have been in the suite sleeping alone. Raina could have been... She slammed a lid on the morbid thoughts and swallowed the fear in her throat. A few hours ago, she was irritated with the inconveniences created by the storm, but now, she was thankful. Her ancestors must have been looking out for her.

"Was it someone from the Nine Dragons? How did you hear about this?" Raina's eyes widened at a sudden thought. "Did...did you authorize the hit?"

"If I authorized the hit, would I be here trying to save your bacon?" Sonny said. "Someone posted it on our chat channel. I don't know who it was because it was hidden behind an alias, but I assumed it was legitimate. The post gave your full name, where you're staying, and a photograph of you."

Raina had no idea when Detective Mars had taken a picture of her. Probably when she was removing the panda head charm from his key ring. Blowing up the honeymoon suite was probably a smart move because it would have also destroyed the data stored in the panda charm. No, he didn't personally do the deed. Instead, he had posted it up on a chat channel. She wondered if the federal government was monitoring this channel. "So, how much am I worth? How much did this person offer for the hit?"

"Two-thousand dollars," Sonny said.

"That's it? That's how much my life is worth?" Raina said. She was offended by the small amount.

"It was supposed to be an easy job."

"What is that supposed to mean?"

"You're tiny and a lightweight. You probably sleep like a pig once you turn in for the night." Sonny shrugged. "An easy job."

"You said you were trying to save me?"

"I was hoping to get here to warn you and move you to a safer location." He raised an eyebrow. "Do you trust me enough to come with me to a safe house?"

"You think someone will try again?"

"I don't know. I had the post removed and the person blocked from the channel, but he could have somebody else repost it for him again."

Raina considered her options. With a failed first attempt, and the post for the hit removed, she probably had some breathing room. There might not even be a second attempt, especially if Detective Mars refused to pay for the explosion because Raina was still alive.

And there was no way she was "disappearing" with Sonny Kwan. She trusted him as much as she did a rabid dog.

"I think I'll pass," Raina said more calmly than she felt.

Her thoughts were racing. What if the next time the hitman came at her when she was with her grandma and her younger brother? But she couldn't just go into hiding to protect herself. Detective Mars probably knew he could get her to cooperate by threatening one of her family members. This would leave her grandma, younger brother, and her great-aunt vulnerable to his malice. Whereas, if Raina went about her business as usual, the hitman would be focused on finding an opportunity to get rid of her instead of her family. And Detective Mars would probably display more caution if he knew the panda head charm was in a safe location.

"Why is someone trying to kill you?" Sonny asked. "Did you find something?"

Raina hesitated. What if this was a setup and Sonny was here to retrieve the panda charm? Time to throw the Nine Dragons off her trail. "I got back my cousin's key charm from Detective Mars."

"What did you do with it? Is it a memory card?"

Raina shrugged, playing the bimbolina card. "I don't know. I'm not very techy. It looks like a cute Japanese thing, but my grandma said you need a code to Bluetooth in. Anyways, we gave it to one of Matthew's contacts." There. This should redirect the Nine Dragons to the feds.

"Who was your contact?" Sonny asked.

Raina shrugged again. "I don't know who the person is. Matthew texted me the location and instructions for the drop-off. We put the panda charm in a package of maxi pads and left it in a restroom stall at the open-air mall." She couldn't believe how easily the lie slipped out.

Sonny studied Raina for a long moment. Finally, he got up and headed toward the door. "Stay out of sight for a bit, Rainy. I'll let Timothy Mars know that you don't have the memory stick anymore."

As the door clicked shut, Raina flopped back onto the bed, giddy with relief. Raina knew that he didn't believe her story despite what Sonny said, but he was willing to take it at face value. She didn't know if it was her husband's doing or if Sonny might really have a tender spot for her. Regardless, she was just glad to get rid of him.

Po Po and Win came into the room through the adjoining door.

"That was a good story, sis," Win said.

Po Po shushed him and went to look out the peephole. She opened the door and glanced up and down the hallway. "All clear," she said, locking up.

The enormity of what just happened hit Raina like a ton of bricks. The explosion in the honeymoon suite probably destroyed all their things. She looked down at the candy cane striped pajamas. She would have to resort to wearing her grandma's pantsuits or purchasing Hawaiian muumuus from the convenience store. She groaned out loud, covering her face with her hands. Sometimes her life resembled a sitcom.

Just as they were about to return to their beds, someone knocked loudly on Po Po's door again. Raina's heart sank. She knew that knock. A quick look through the peephole confirmed it was Sonny Kwan again. She opened the door with a sigh.

"Now what?" she said, folding her arms across her chest.

Sonny gave her a sheepish look. "A tree fell across the main road out of the resort grounds. There's no way in or out. Can I crash here for the night?"

"Are you kidding me?" Raina said. One of her ancestors really had a twisted sense of humor.

"With the power outage, I can't get a room from the front desk," Sonny said. "The computer system is off for the night and will need to be manually rebooted in the morning."

Raina frowned. She glanced at the lights in the

hallway and the desk lamp in the room. They were significantly dimmer than usual, but she thought they were on night mode. Maybe the lights were on generator mode. "Can't you just sleep in your car?"

Sonny gave her a look like she grew another head. "I come out of my way, in this storm, to save your behind, and you want me to sleep in the car? It's dark and cold outside." He brushed past her and marched into the room. "So, where do I sleep?"

Po Po winked at him and patted the bed. "We can be roommates tonight. I can keep you nice and toasty."

Raina rolled her eyes and locked the door. Didn't her grandma know that sleeping with the enemy wasn't a good idea?

Raina glanced at her smartwatch. It was already three in the morning. She doubted that she would fall asleep again with Sonny in the room. It would be like trying to sleep while sitting on the edge of a cliff.

Sonny glanced at Po Po on the bed. "I was hoping for a different bedmate."

"In your dreams," Raina muttered to herself. She reached for her pillow. "I can bunk up with Win." She pointed at Po Po. "Just keep the animal noises down. I still want to get some sleep."

Sonny's gaze flickered between Raina and Po Po. He made a beeline for Win's room. "Looks like we're sharing the bed for the night, bro."

Win sat up in bed and gave Raina a look like this situation was all her fault. He grabbed the comforter and pillow, strolled into Po Po's room, and made a nest for himself in front of the adjoining doorway.

"Hey, what am I going to use for a blanket?" Sonny said.

"Get creative. Good night," Win said to Sonny and locked the adjoining door.

18

A CLEAR PICTURE

Raina got a few hours of sleep after all. When she woke at the crack of dawn, her eyes were gummy, and she had a mild headache. She was also hungry—the instant noodle cup was a distant memory—and with the blocked road, she was worried they might not have food again today.

While Raina brushed her teeth at the sink next to her grandma, she whispered, "Po Po, what did you do with the panda charm? We have to keep it safe until we get it into Matthew's hands."

Po Po patted her right hip. "It's in my underwear," she whispered back with her toothbrush hanging out of her mouth.

Raina blinked. Her brain was a little slow this morning, but it wasn't turned off. Her grandma was eccentric, but she wasn't a loony tune. Storing something in a person's undies was just too gross. "Did you say underwear?"

"There's a little pocket on the side, just big enough for small items like a key or a credit card," Po Po said. "I am one of the backers for the design. It's mighty convenient for hiding small things. Remind me to get you a couple of pairs when we get home."

For half a heartbeat, Raina didn't know what to say. She wasn't surprised her grandma would be attracted to the design. "Just don't drop it in the toilet when you go to the restroom. Water and electronic devices don't play well together."

"Don't worry. There's a zipper."

Raina snorted. Including a small pocket and mini zipper in underwear was a brilliant idea. It was an even safer hiding place than the bra.

Po Po rinsed her mouth and turned to Raina. "They will have to strip-search me to find it." She paused a minute thoughtfully. "It's been a while since I was last strip-searched. Boy, he was a hunk." She playfully fanned her face with her hand.

Raina choked on the toothpaste. Yuck! She didn't need this image in her head before coffee.

A few minutes later, Raina was dressed in one of her grandma's turquoise tracksuits with her flip-flop sandals. Though the styling was considered retro nowadays, she had a feeling the tracksuit was actually from the 1980s. The velour fabric had faded patches at the elbows and knees.

Unfortunately, with the resort running on generator power, laundry wasn't an option. If Raina was lucky, maybe she could find a T-shirt at the convenience store. She pulled her hair back into a tight bun to hide her signature curly hair.

She should check on the honeymoon suite, but with the explosion and the heavy rain, there probably wasn't anything worth salvaging. And there was the possibility that someone might be watching the room and looking for a curly haired Chinese woman.

Raina and Po Po left Win snoring in the room to head downstairs. At six in the morning, the only people up and about were the resort staff. Usually, Raina would run on the treadmill in the fitness room at this hour.

Being married to a man who got paid to stay in shape was tough. Even though Raina didn't suffer from self-esteem issues, she still felt the need to maintain the status quo. This meant getting up at the crack of dawn to run in circles like a hamster on a wheel.

The Wayfarer restaurant was still closed. The same sign from the night before was taped on the door.

Po Po took one look at the sign, spun on her heels, and marched across the lobby to knock on the office door. "Hey, May! Open up."

Auntie May opened the office door and waved them in. She had eye bags the size of coconuts. Her Hawaiian muumuu was creased like she had slept in it. Raina flicked a glance at the recliner in the corner of the room. The blanket was bunched up in the middle of the seat. Yep, her great-aunt had slept in the office last night.

"No one has seen Leilani since yesterday at the bar," Auntie May said, sinking into her swivel chair. "I don't know where that girl is hiding. We have fifty people at the resort, including the staff, who need food in about an hour or so. At times like this, I wish I had sold the resort a few years ago. We could have taken the money and run."

"Why didn't you sell it?" Raina asked.

"This property has been in my family for three generations," Auntie May said. "I was holding onto it for the grandchildren. It's their heritage." She sighed. "Ailani didn't understand this. It is the reason why she was estranged from the family. She wanted to sell the land, divide everything up, and all of us go our own separate ways. But the resort is holding us together as a family. The luaus help us pass on the stories, the dances, and songs to the next generation. I can't give this up without a fight."

"We heard about the tree blocking the main road. Is someone coming to take care of it?" Po Po asked.

Auntie May shook her head. "The road is our private road, and I can't get a tree-cutting service to answer my call."

Raina doubted that Auntie May would find someone any time soon. With the rest of the town in probably the same condition, why would Auntie May's dilapidated resort get to the top of the priority list? If Raina owned a tree-cutting service, she would make sure the big, fancy resorts could resumed operations before anyone else. After all, they had bigger wallets.

"Is the power line down?" Raina asked.

Auntie May nodded. "I called the power company. A 21kV line is down somewhere outside the resort, so the whole area doesn't have power. It might take a couple of days to repair it. Luckily, Leilani insisted we replace the generators last year, so we have power for basic stuff for about two days. We can't do laundry though because the dryers use too much energy."

"Can't your landscaping guy do something about the tree across the road?" Raina said.

Auntie May stared at Raina in disbelief. "Have you met the landscaper? He is five years older than me. He might have a heart attack from the suggestion alone."

"He doesn't have to do the work," Po Po said. "Just supervise it. Do you have chainsaws?"

Auntie May shrugged. "I really don't know what the landscaping crew have in their shed."

Raina remembered seeing several cars parked on the gravel lot of the staff housing building. "Has someone tried to leave the resort from the road by the staff housing?"

"It connects to the same blocked road," Auntie May said. "There is only one main road in and out of the resort."

Raina shivered at the comment. They were trapped

at the resort with a triad boss and potentially her cousin's killer. She couldn't do anything about the bad folks, but she could do something about food. She shifted her attention back to the discussion. "Why was the restaurant closed last night? Was it the freezer?"

Auntie May nodded. "I thought Leilani called the repair person, but she didn't. And now he can't even come out here." She rubbed her temples as if in pain. "All the food will go bad."

"I'm sure we can salvage something," Raina said. "As long as the door is closed, we can still eat the food in the freezer today. But what will we do tomorrow?"

"After we move the tree aside, we can send Win and some staff out to make a supply run." Po Po flapped a hand in Raina's direction. "Go work your magic. See what you can whip up for breakfast and lunch."

Raina raised an eyebrow. Po Po thought the gap between the refrigerator and the stove was the Grand Canyon. When her grandma had lived in San Francisco, she had a personal cook. Po Po didn't understand that a person couldn't just whip something up for a crowd. It took a lot more planning and effort. "I still need help in the kitchen. Where are the kitchen staff?"

"Everyone went home last night," Auntie May said. "Only the head cook lives at the staff housing in 1C. I called him this morning, but he's not picking up. And the rest of the staff can't come in because of the blocked road."

Raina's stomach growled. "Okay, I'll have someone

make a coffee and tea bar in the lobby. Then, after breakfast, I'll go knock on the cook's door and peek in on Leilani's apartment."

Auntie May opened a drawer and pulled out a set of keys. "These are the restaurant keys. We lock up the pantry and the alcohol. Here's the spare key to Leilani's apartment." She handed Raina the keys. "Thank you so much, my dear. I don't know what has gotten into Leilani."

Raina knew what happened to her cousin, but she had to keep silent until the official channel figured it out. Did running a resort overwhelm Ailani? Was this why she was in hiding mode? What was her motive for pretending to be her sister in the first place?

Auntie May gave Po Po a shaky smile. "I am so glad you came out here, Bonnie. I don't know what I would have done without you." Her eyes filled up with tears. "I am so sorry. I don't know what is wrong with me. I feel so defeated."

Po Po patted Auntie May's hand. "Let us take a load off your shoulders. That's what family is for. Radio the landscaper and get him in here. If we throw enough manpower at it, we can clear enough of the main road to get a car through." She looked at Raina. "Go work your magic in the kitchen, girl. Make me proud."

Forty minutes later, Raina and a resort staff had set up the breakfast bar in the lobby. Luckily, there was plenty of food in the pantry. Breakfast consisted of grab-and-go stuff like bagels, toast, and packaged muffins. However, the only spreads available were peanut butter and jelly. The cream cheese and milk had gone bad.

As for lunch, Raina had found deli meat, sliced cheese, and several bags of lettuce. She instructed the resort staff to clean up the breakfast bar at ten o'clock and lay out food for a sandwich bar at eleven. Since the food was free, Raina didn't think the guests would complain too loudly. It wasn't like they had other options for food.

Win came downstairs and made a beeline for the food. "Can you pack some to go, Sis? Po Po and the landscaper dudes are already working on the downed tree. I think there are three other guys with them. That's all the male staff at the resort. We were lucky they couldn't leave after their shift last night."

Raina went into the kitchen and packed some bagels, muffins, a coffee carafe, and bottled water in a cardboard box. She added to-go cups, sugar, and half-and-half.

Win came into the kitchen with a bagel in one hand and a cup of tea in the other. "What's for lunch?"

Raina rolled her eyes. "You haven't even finished breakfast yet."

Win shrugged. "Just trying to see if I need to save a bagel for later. I don't want a repeat of last night."

"We will have sandwiches for lunch." Yawning, Raina refilled her coffee cup. If only she could sneak upstairs for a few more hours of sleep. "Is Sonny still in your room?"

Win shook his head. "He was already gone when I woke up."

Raina hadn't seen Sonny in the lobby area, but she had been busy. Even if he was lurking somewhere in the resort, he probably wouldn't harm her, or she would already be dead. She dismissed Sonny from her mind.

And with the trees blocking the entrance to the resort, she was probably safe from Detective Mars for now. It would be more productive to focus her attention on finding Ailani and the murderer.

Win stuffed the last bite of the bagel in his mouth. "See you in a bit, Sis. I have a feeling I am the gofer for the team."

As Win strolled off holding the box of food, Raina's cell phone chirped with an incoming message. It was from her grandma about the hotel video feed. The message was sent fifteen minutes ago.

HACKER WENT THROUGH THE HOTEL'S VIDEO. JENNY AND BIG MAC SPOKE FOR THIRTY MINUTES AT 3 AM TWO NIGHTS BEFORE LEILANI'S DEATH AT THE STAFF PARKING LOT. FOUND MR. MOLEY MOLE. NO AUDIO.

Raina stared at the message and clicked on the link. Her grandma's hacker had clipped out the relevant video and uploaded it to a cloud storage.

The video was dim, mostly shadows. There was only the ambient light from the resort. A woman stepped out of the shadows, and her face was illuminated for a fraction of a second before disappearing back into the shadows. It was Jenny Harris.

As Big Mac headed toward his truck, Jenny must have called out to him. He stopped, and they chatted. Raina zoomed in, but she couldn't make out the expressions on their faces. The two of them got into the truck, and they peeled out of the parking lot. Maybe Big Mac was upset by their conversation. There was no video clip of when Jenny returned to the resort. When she returned, did she hide her face?

What did Jenny and Big Mac talk about? Did it have something to do with the car accident in high school? Was this enough for Big Mac to murder the woman he claimed to be in love with? Or were the two of them in cahoots?

Raina clicked on the second link in the text message. It was another video clip taken last time Raina saw her cousin. The camera was set up above the entrance of the bar.

In the video, Raina walked away from Leilani toward the entrance. In the background, Leilani was on the phone with an empty cocktail glass in front of her. Mr. Moley Mole—the blond bartender in a Hawaiian shirt and black slack—set another Leilani drink on a tray. He pushed his aviator-framed glasses up his nose and strolled over to Leilani.

Mr. Moley Mole slid another cocktail glass onto the table—one with a red paper umbrella on it. He kept his face down and angled away from the camera.

Leilani took a large gulp and chatted for a few minutes on the phone. With the phone still glued to her ear, she stood on wobbly legs. She appeared to look around, confused. She took another gulp of the cocktail and said something to Mr. Moley Mole. He opened the side door and waved for Leilani to come over. Leilani stumbled but made her way to the door.

The side door was primarily used in the mornings for deliveries to the bar and restaurant. At that time of the day, no one would be out there. A guest would have to make an effort to walk around the main building to see the side door and the hidden delivery driveway. It was the perfect spot to temporarily hide a body.

Was her cousin drunk already? Or had she been drugged? The side door slammed closed by itself, and Mr. Moley Mole strolled to the bar entrance. He kept his head turned away from the camera, exposing the side of his neck and the reddish thumbprint underneath his earlobe—like the red birthmark on Jenny Harris's neck.

19

A BLAST FROM THE PAST

Raina glanced up from her cell phone screen, not seeing the lobby in front of her. Several conflicting thoughts whirled in her mind. Though Jenny had tried to hide her brown hair underneath a blonde wig and to dress like a man, she had forgotten to cover up her birthmark. If Raina hadn't noticed it at the ER waiting room, she would have continued to look for Mr. Moley Mole.

Jenny had given Leilani a drugged cocktail that probably incapacitated her cousin. Instead of following Leilani to the side door, Jenny went back to the lobby, through the pool area, and to the rental shack to establish her alibi. After all, no one would check the area behind the side door until the next morning.

And when Jenny came back later to move the body, she tossed the cocktail behind the kukui tree, thinking no one would connect the broken glass with the murder. With all the guests going back and forth from the resort, the pool, the luau, and the rental shack, there were probably plenty of broken cocktail glasses.

Jenny probably had murdered Leilani to avenge Sarah's death. Raina assumed Jenny knew exactly which twin to kill, and it was Auntie May who had mistaken the identity of the victim. Even though Ailani had pretended to be her sister at the resort, Jenny didn't appear to be interested in the younger twin.

But why did Jenny target the older twin? Did Leilani drive that night, supply the alcohol, or both? What triggered Jenny to kill Leilani now? Was it the anniversary of her sister's death?

But what about the late night conversation between Big Mac and Jenny? What did they discuss? The Leilani drink was created by Big Mac, and Raina had no reason to believe that Jenny knew how to mix it. Hence, Big Mac must have made the drink before heading into the kitchen, but as an experienced bartender, why would he leave a drink unattended, especially if it was meant for his lady love? Did Jenny convince Big Mac to help her during their late night chat? Were they in cahoots?

Raina left the resort staff in charge of handling the coffee and breakfast bar. She strode across the lobby and knocked on the office door again.

Auntie May opened the door.

"I got breakfast and lunch sorted out," Raina said.

She told her great-aunt the food plan. "Did Big Mac stay over last night? It might be a good idea to have the bar open around lunch. The alcohol might keep people distracted, so they don't think about being trapped at the resort. It will also bring in some revenue."

"Yes, he stayed over last night in one of the empty rooms," Auntie May said. "It's a little too early to call him now, but I'll do it later."

"Have you been able to reach the head cook or Ai—Leilani?" Raina stumbled over her cousin's name. It wasn't hard to keep them straight in Raina's mind, but it was difficult remembering who knew Ailani wasn't officially dead.

"No. I wonder if the phone line is down, and cell service is sketchy even at the best of times." Auntie May handed Raina a walkie-talkie. "The resort uses channel eight."

The number eight was considered a lucky number in Chinese culture because it was a homonym for wealth. So Raina was not surprised Auntie May used this channel for her resort business.

"Here's the oddest thing—the hotel video cameras are malfunctioning," Auntie May said. "Even the hard drives were wiped."

"What do you mean malfunctioning?" Raina asked. "It's not recording anything?"

Auntie May shook her head. "The system is ten years old, but I didn't think a storm could zap it and knock out all the cameras. This didn't happen in previous storms."

Raina didn't believe for a minute that the storm did this to the cameras. One or two, maybe. But all of them? No, this was sabotage. And wasn't Jenny a cinematographer? She would know her way around cameras.

"I'm heading upstairs to get Big Mac and then to the staff housing," Raina said. She asked nonchalantly, "What room is Jenny Harris in?"

Auntie May frowned. "We normally don't give out this information, but I'll do it for you." She tapped on the computer screen. "Room 320."

"Auntie May, I know Leilani was in a car accident that killed someone in their last year of high school. Can you tell me more about it?"

Auntie May's face closed in. "You should probably ask Leilani. I don't like talking about that period in her life. It's something that still haunts both girls."

And also haunts Jenny Harris, Raina thought. "What happened that night might be relevant to what is happening now. Were both of the twins in the car? Who was the driver? And how did the girls get the alcohol?"

Auntie May rubbed her temples and closed her eyes for a long moment as if in prayer. "Both girls were in the car that night, and they told the police that Leilani was the driver."

Raina had a sinking feeling in the pit of her stomach. "Ailani was the driver, wasn't she?"

"Yes. How did you know?"

Raina sighed inwardly. Leilani wasn't the driver, and Jenny had killed the wrong twin. "Just a hunch. Why did Leilani take the fall for her sister?"

"Ailani was a terror in her teenage years. She had just gotten out of juvenile hall again. And I guess Leilani didn't want her sister back there again."

Raina wasn't sure she would make the same call in a similar situation. However, all three girls were drunk, and it was easy enough to make some bad judgment calls. "And you were okay with this?"

"I didn't know about the switch-a-roo until years later. By that time, it was too late."

"How did Sarah die?" Raina asked. "I heard she was thrown into the ravine."

"It was a horrible accident. Sarah slipped and fell."

Raina's eyes widened. What other details did Jenny get wrong?

Auntie May continued with the story. "It was dark, and there was a light rain. The car went around a curve too fast, and Ailani hit a tree growing on the edge of the road. The tree prevented the car from falling into the ravine. It was a hundred-foot drop."

"Then what happened?"

"The girls were too impaired to realize the danger. All three of them ran out of the car to look at the damage. Except Sarah slipped on the wet dirt and fell off the edge."

Raina shuddered at the mental image. It was all a horrible accident. Her cousin hadn't directly caused Sarah's death, but Jenny had felt otherwise. "But the Harris family didn't see this as an accident?"

"They blamed Leilani for everything. Lawyers got involved, but eventually the case was thrown out."

"What was Leilani's punishment?"

"A few months in juvenile hall and community work. It took two years of therapy before Leilani eventually moved on from the accident. Ailani disappeared for a while."

Raina could see why the Harris family felt the punishment wasn't enough to make up for losing their daughter. And since the parents had no recourse in the legal system, they had fed a lie to Jenny instead, placing all the blame on Leilani.

"Does anyone else know that Ailani was the driver that night?" Raina asked.

Auntie May shook her head. "Just the three of us. I still second guess the decision to keep quiet about it, but Leilani already got her punishment. But Ailani always felt guilty that her sister took her place. After their parents' deaths, Ailani turned to petty crime, while Leilani turned to alcohol. I didn't recognize any of the signs until it was too late."

Raina patted Auntie May's hand. "It wasn't your fault. You did the best you could with what you were given. If it was anyone's fault, then it was the ancestors' fault for not looking out for the family."

"Leilani has been in and out of rehab over the years," Auntie May said. "She's been sober going on for three years now, thank goodness."

Raina blinked. Yikes! Her great-aunt didn't know Leilani was back off the wagon again, enough so she even had a cocktail named after her. Big Mac had known the family long enough to know Leilani was an alcoholic. Did he do this intentionally? What was his end game?

RAINA HUGGED Auntie May and left her great-aunt to call Big Mac to open the bar for lunch. Once in the lobby again, she used the walkie-talkie to talk to her grandma.

"I have the volume up so Win can hear. He is driving," Po Po said.

"Did the landscapers move the tree?" Raina asked.

"They're making progress. But the head landscaper felt I was more trouble than help." Po Po harrumphed. "He gave us the ultimatum. Either we leave, or he does. So, we are on our way back to the resort."

Raina smirked, glad that her grandma couldn't see her expression. She could hear her brother snickering in the background.

"That's a man for you," Po Po continued. "Doesn't know a woman's worth until she's gone."

"Rainy," Win called out. "Po Po saw a couple of harmless water snakes and ran around screaming like a chicken with her head cut off. She knocked over all the food. That's why the head landscaper wanted her gone from the job site."

"Oh, no. Do they need more food?" Raina said. "I can pack another box for them."

"Don't worry about it," Win said. "You did a good job wrapping everything in plastic wrap."

"They were not harmless snakes, Rainy," Po Po said. "They were as thick as my thumb. Good thing I wore boots. I don't want them snakes biting my ankles. They are already swollen enough as it is."

Raina was glad she wasn't babysitting her grandma. "I could use some help to track down Ailani." She summarized her conversation with Auntie May. "We need to convince Ailani to hide until the authorities can get Jenny behind bars. I'm afraid that once Jenny finds out Ailani was the driver that night, she might be next..." Her voice trailed off.

The hair on the back of Raina's neck stiffened, and her gaze scanned the lobby. More people were in the lobby now, most of them gathering at the breakfast bar. Two couples stood in line to talk to the front desk. Nothing seemed out of place, but a sense of unease settled between Raina's shoulder blades.

"Rainy?" Po Po said through the cell phone. "Are you still there?"

Raina took a deep breath. She was probably feeling jumpy because of the situation. Who wanted to be trapped someplace with a murderer? "Yes, I got distracted."

"By what?"

"It's nothing, but I felt someone watching me."

"Who is it?" Po Po asked, her voice filled with concern.

Raina shrugged even though her grandma couldn't see her. "I don't know. And it's gone now."

"Just be careful," Po Po said. "Detective Mars will need proof that Jenny is Leilani's killer."

"I'm not going to that man for anything. I can't believe he got someone to blow up the honeymoon suite. I could have been inside."

"Oh, yeah. I almost forgot about that. I haven't seen the damage, so it doesn't feel real to me. Do you want me to check it out for you?"

Raina thought about her grandma's offer. Po Po and Win were probably safe enough since their photos weren't circulated online. But there wasn't any urgency to survey the damages. "It can wait. We'll need a confession from Jenny first and then get this information to the authorities."

"Maybe we should send Win to do the job."

"I don't think that's a good idea," Raina said slowly. Her brother had been silent throughout this conversation. Was he still in denial that Jenny was the killer? What if he wanted to "save the damsel in distress?"

"We can wire Win up and have him show Jenny the video clips from my hacker," Po Po said. "Let's see how she explains the situation."

"I don't know," Raina said.

Win might have the body of a grown-up, but sometimes he still acted like a teenager. Raina would be insane to leave him alone with a cold-blooded killer.

But then again, he would be the perfect person to get a confession from Jenny. She might even be lulled into thinking she could get him to help her.

"I can do it, Sis," Win called out. He sounded resigned.

"Oh, all right," Raina said with reluctance.

"Yes!" Po Po shouted.

Raina cringed and moved the phone away from her ear. She could hear Po Po whooping and giving Win a high five. The whole investigation was a game to her grandma. Raina was starting to have misgivings about the plan.

"I need to get out to the staff housing to check on the head cook and Ailani," Raina said.

"What if Jenny already kidnapped Ailani and stashed her somewhere at the resort?" Po Po asked.

Raina didn't even want to think of this possibility. While it would be poetic justice for Ailani to get kidnapped after her stunt a few days ago, Raina didn't want anything to happen to her cousin. "Before we go down that path, let me knock on her door first."

"And we'll get ready in our rooms," Po Po said. "I'll have Win wired and ready to go by the time you get back here."

"Po Po, how are you able to get all your spy gear through the airport security?"

"That's need-to-know, Rainy. And you don't need to know."

Raina rolled her eyes and clipped the walkie talkie to her waistband. Her cell phone chirped, and she pulled it out of her purse. It was a text message from Matthew sent last night.

Someone posted a hit on you online. Don't go back to the honeymoon suite.

Raina snorted at the irony. Once again, an important message came too late to be of any use. But at least she knew the Nine Dragons's secret chat channel was being monitored by the government. And it also meant Matthew was on his way back to the resort. He would never leave her to deal with this dangerous situation alone.

The knot between her shoulder blades loosened. Her husband was still too far away to do anything to help, but he was aware of the situation and on his way back to the resort. This was enough for Raina to feel like she had backup...competent backup.

20

AN UNEXPECTED HELPER

Raina had expected the trail to be a mess with toppled trees and flooding. Instead, a light blanket of fern and broken branches covered several spots on the narrow dirt path. At about the halfway mark, a tree lay across the trail, and Raina scrambled over the three-foot diameter. Now that she had gone through the rainforest for the third time, it was starting to look more familiar and less foreign. It took twenty-five minutes to get through the rainforest to the staff housing complex.

The concrete box with the metal railings looked even more depressing under the gray sky and misty rain. No laundry flapped on the balconies today. Raina strolled around to the front of the building. A big tree branch blocked the driveway of the gravel parking lot. She pulled out the walkie-talkie and spoke to Auntie May, letting her know about the tree.

"The men are cutting the branches off the fallen tree on the main road," Auntie May said through the walkie-talkie. "The head landscaper thinks they can get a vehicle through by lunchtime and have the rest cleared out by this evening. The staff will have to walk through the rainforest in the meantime."

They said their goodbyes, and Raina marched to the head cook's apartment unit. The head cook opened the door on the first knock. It was the man who had threatened Raina with a metal ladle when she was in the restaurant kitchen the other day.

"Yes?" the head cook said, arms crossed. His body blocked the doorway.

As if Raina wanted to go inside. "Auntie May wants to know if you can put together dinner for the fifty people at the resort."

"I can't cook without fresh food," the head cook said. "I make my meals from scratch. What am I supposed to make? Spaghetti?"

Raina wanted to tell the man to get off his high horse. There were jars of Ragu sauce and spaghetti noodles in the pantry. "Just try your best. We are aiming for filling food rather than gourmet cuisine. People can't leave the resort, and they can't cook in their rooms."

"What about lunch?" he asked sullenly.

"We got that figured out," Raina said. "We are having deli meat sandwiches."

The head cook wrinkled his nose. "I want nothing

to do with that. I'll be in the kitchen at three to start the dinner service."

"Just to let you know, the road out of the parking lot is blocked. So you'll have to walk through the rainforest, but there is also a tree blocking the path."

The head cook looked at Raina like it was all her fault. "How am I supposed to get over the tree?"

"You can walk around the tree or climb over it. Just take your time."

"What if I slip and fall? Will I get worker's comp?"

"You're not the wicked witch," Raina said through clenched teeth. "You won't melt in the rain."

Raina left the man standing in the doorway. She'd had enough of his attitude. Sure, he was the most important person in the kitchen, but it was his job to show up for work. And if he didn't want to work, Raina could make spaghetti with the jars of Ragu. Geez.

By the time Raina got to Leilani's front door, she had calmed down. Usually, it took a lot more than a prissy person to get her worked up. Was it the weather? She just didn't have her normal patience.

In the back of Raina's mind, a ticking clock was counting down. If she took too long at the staff housing complex, her grandma and brother might go to Jenny's room by themselves. And who knew what mischief the two of them could get into without Raina's supervision?

When Raina knocked on Leilani's door, there was

no answer. She called Leilani's landline but got the answering machine. She hung up and knocked again.

"Ailani," Raina called out. "I know you're pretending to be Leilani. I'm coming in. Auntie May gave me a spare key."

Raina waited for a minute with her ear pressed to the door, but she didn't hear anyone coming to answer the knock. Glancing around the landing area, she inserted the key and went inside the apartment.

The smell was the first thing that hit her. A pungent, greasy smell like a bag of french fries left in a car on a hot summer day. Yuck! Raina blinked, giving her eyes time to adjust to the dim light. She crossed the room and yanked open the vertical vinyl blinds to let in the faint daylight. She opened a couple of windows, hoping the air circulation would help get rid of the smell.

Raina turned from the window to survey the studio. Unlike the last time she was here, the place was a pigsty. Takeout cartons and bags littered every horizontal surface in the apartment—someone needed to take out the trash.

Ailani's apartment didn't look anything like this. Maybe her cousin had holed up here to avoid seeing people who might know her sister. Or perhaps she didn't care because she was grieving. After all, staying in Leilani's apartment and being surrounded by Leilani's things had to be difficult. No matter their differences, the two of them were siblings and twins on top of that. Maybe Ailani regretted her decision to impersonate her sister but didn't know how to get out of it.

Raina did a quick search of the apartment. There was no indication that Ailani was gone for good, but there was nothing to suggest she would be back anytime soon. Raina couldn't just wait here. It could be hours or even days.

Raina had no way of directly communicating with Ailani since it would require too much explanation or even an outright lie to ask for her cousin's cell phone number. Instead, she pulled out a small notebook from her purse and scribbled a note warning her cousin that Jenny Harris might be Leilani's killer.

PLEASE KEEP YOURSELF HIDDEN UNTIL THE AUTHORITIES ARREST JENNY. IF SHE KNOWS YOU WERE THE DRIVER THE NIGHT THAT HER SISTER DIED, SHE MIGHT COME AFTER YOU.

She scribbled her name and cell phone number at the bottom of the sheet. She glanced around the apartment. Where could she put this note so it wouldn't get lost in the mess? She grabbed a piece of tape from the desk next to the bed and taped the white sheet of paper to the middle of the black TV screen.

Raina locked up and dialed her grandma's cell phone number. The call went straight to voicemail.

"I'm heading back to the resort," Raina said into

her phone. "Wait for me." She power walked down the staircase.

A few minutes later, Raina was inside the rainforest again, trotting back to the resort on the narrow dirt path. The rain forest amplified the patter of the light rain on the trees and foliage, and the ravine gurgled with moving water. They drowned out all the other sounds. Raina could barely hear her wet flip-flop sandals slapping against her foot. Where did the wild chickens roost in this storm?

Raina was climbing over the downed tree when the hair on the back of her neck stiffened. She fell on the trunk with her legs straddling the three-foot diameter kukui tree, and her toes scraped the bark. She yelped in pain. One of her flip-flop sandals fell onto the fern grove next to the dirt path and disappeared from view.

Jenny stepped out from behind a kukui tree. "Raina, I have been waiting for you. We need to talk."

Raina was a sitting duck, and she didn't even have on proper shoes to run away. "Right now is not a good time. How did you know where to find me?"

"I saw you in the lobby, so I followed you," Jenny said. She smiled, a friendly girl-next-door smile. "Then I got tired. I figured you'd have to come back this way sooner or later."

Raina wasn't fooled for one second. Her heart pounded against her chest. "What do you want to talk about?"

"I know who killed Ailani."

Raina blinked at Jenny in confusion. If Jenny was the killer, wouldn't she know which twin had actually died? Or was this some kind of trick? "Why are you telling me this? You should go to the police with the information," Raina said, hoping to stall for time. Her grandma would eventually realize that Raina didn't return to the resort.

"Win told me that you often helped your husband on his investigations. I don't trust Detective Mars, but I think I can trust you."

Raina wanted to strangle her brother. He couldn't just keep his trap shut. Like their grandmother, he probably exaggerated things for attention. "That is not true. I work at a senior center and part-time at a café. I don't have time to poke my nose in other people's business."

Jenny frowned. "I thought Ailani Wong was your cousin."

Raina frowned. There it was again. Either Jenny was a good actress, or she really thought Ailani had died.

The walkie-talkie in Raina's purse crackled to life. "Rainy, are you there?" Her grandma's voice came through loud and clear. "We are ready for Operation Bad Girlfriend. And Mars has landed at the resort."

Jenny gave Raina a quizzical glance. "I hope I'm not the bad girlfriend."

The walkie-talkie crackled again, and Po Po said,

"Win is all wired up to get a confession from Jenny Harris."

Jenny took a step towards Raina, curling her hands into fists. "Are you kidding me? I am trying to help you, and you think I'm the murderer?"

Raina reached inside her purse and turned on the digital recorder app on her phone. Even if Jenny didn't kill Leilani, she was still up to no good. After all, innocent people didn't disguise themselves and pretended to work at the victim's family business unless there was a reason. Maybe Raina could get some kind of confession from Jenny. And if something terrible happened to Raina, the conversation would get backed up to the cloud. Po Po could get her hacker friend to get a copy of the recorded conversation.

Raina made a show of pulling out the walkie-talkie, turning off the volume, dropping it back inside her bag. "You are mistaken. Win wants you to admit that you are in love with him, too." The lie rolled smoothly off Raina's tongue, but she didn't think Jenny bought it.

They were both silent for a long moment, letting the patter of the rain fill the space between them.

Raina's legs were starting to feel numb from straddling the downed tree. The velour tracksuit did little to keep out the rain, and she shivered from the cold. She wanted nothing more than to slide down the tree and run back to the staff housing complex, but she had to keep Jenny talking.

Jenny threw her hands up into the air. "Whatever."

Raina wiggled her foot, hoping to get rid of the pins and needles feeling. "We have the hotel video of you disguised as a man, giving Leilani a drugged cocktail. You also encouraged her to exit the building through the side door by the bar. She probably collapsed after you closed the door, and you went back to the rental shack to establish your alibi. Then you came back later and moved Leilani to the underground oven at the beach."

Jenny shook her head. "What kind of detective are you? You got the details all wrong. Ailani was the twin who died in the underground oven. I don't know what happened to her, but it has nothing to do with me. I admit—I did put Rohypnol in Leilani's cocktail, but she seems to be okay."

"Why did you give my cousin the date-rape drug?"

"I only wanted to talk to her," Jenny said. "I need to know what happened on the night my sister died."

"So you incapacitate someone because she was ignoring you?"

"Okay, maybe I wanted to punish Leilani a little bit. She killed my sister and barely got any jail time. And to make it worse, she's drinking again. So it's only a matter of time before she ruins someone else's life. Maybe it'll scare her straight to black out."

Raina agreed that the penalty for drunk driving wasn't severe enough in most cases, but it didn't mean Jenny could take matters into her own hands.

"When we got back from the ER yesterday afternoon, Leilani walked right past me again," Jenny said. "Even though I waved to her. I understand that she might be mad about the cocktail, but come on. I only did it because she kept ignoring me."

Raina blinked. Jenny had no idea that Leilani was dead. Or that the drugged cocktail had given the killer an opportunity to get rid of her cousin. "Do you think what you did was no big deal?"

"Nothing happened to her. She just took a long..." Jenny said, pausing for a moment to consider her words. "Nap."

Raina would like to know what a judge would think about this long nap. Geez. "What about the disguise?"

Jenny squirmed uncomfortably, shifting her weight from one foot to the other. "Leilani recognized me the first day I checked in. Apparently, I look just like Sarah. Without a disguise, I can't even get close to Leilani."

Raina stared at Jenny for a long moment. She didn't know what to say. It was one thing to pretend to be a bimbolina, but quite another to actually be a self-centered bimbolina. Win was lucky his little crush on Jenny didn't go any further than it did. "Did Big Mac also recognize you? We also got video of the two of you driving off somewhere in the middle of the night."

"Where are you getting all these videos? I thought I erased all of them."

"That's need-to-know. And you don't need to know." Raina smirked. She had been dying to say these lines to someone after hearing them from everyone else. "Why did you seek out Big Mac in the middle of the night?"

Jenny shrugged. "I wanted to hear what happened to him after my sister's death. He refused to talk to me during work hours, so I had to seek him out after his shift. He had dated my sister since freshman year in high school. He was a foster child, and we were his only family."

Raina considered Jenny's words. Everyone thought they were Big Mac's family. However, Raina had never heard Big Mac refer to anyone as family, including Auntie May. The bartender appeared to fit whatever role was expected of him.

And speaking of the devil, Big Mac came up behind Jenny and smashed a bottle of vodka on her head. Jenny's eyes rolled up, and she dropped to the ground. Big Mac shook his index finger at Raina. "Didn't I warn you about the cat?"

21

MUD WRESTLE

Time seemed to slow down. Jenny fell to the ground with the grace of a broken ballerina. Raina stared in shock and horror at the blood pooling next to the younger woman's head. She lifted her gaze and met Big Mac's arctic-blue eyes. A shard of ice settled on Raina's chest, spreading to the rest of her body. How did she not see this coming? Jenny had been telling the truth all along. She had been an unwitting accomplice.

"Why?" Raina finally said, her heart pounding against her chest. "I thought you were in love with Leilani."

"How can I be in love with the person who ruined my life?" Big Mac said. "Leilani killed the only person who ever loved me. I had been in the foster system since I was three days old. I had been in twenty-three homes by the time I was in high school. Sarah was the only person who actually cared about me and believed in my potential."

All the pieces finally snapped into place for Raina. "You named a drink after Leilani because you wanted her to fall off the wagon again. You wanted her to self-destruct. But it was taking too long, wasn't it?"

Big Mac raised an eyebrow. "You're smarter than you look. When Jenny told me about her plan, I knew it was the opportunity I had been waiting for. I hid Leilani in the cart I use to deliver supplies to the tiki bar. No one even questioned why I had a tablecloth covering it. And when the cook came back from checking the imu, I knew I had an hour to take care of business."

"Sarah slipped and fell. No one killed her. It was a horrible accident. You killed an innocent woman."

Big Mac ignored Raina's comment. "Leilani was the reason why I lost my college scholarship. She was the reason why I am stuck working for her family. If I wasn't grieving for Sarah, I wouldn't have gotten injured."

Raina shivered at the chill in Big Mac's tone. He truly believed that his misfortune was someone else's fault rather than his addiction to opioids. What happened to personal responsibility?

Big Mac's hands snaked out and clamped onto Raina's ankle. She tried kicking at him but only managed to wiggle her foot. One quick tug, and Raina slid off the tree trunk. Down, down she went until she fell onto the puddle next to Big Mac's feet.

As mud splashed against Raina's face and the impact forced the air out of her chest, she grunted at the pain. She tried to scramble up, but her legs felt like wet noodles. So she rolled onto her side, hoping to put some distance between her body and Big Mac's foot. A well-timed kick could do some serious damage to her petite frame, but a well-placed kick to the crotch could also do some serious damage to the bartender.

Big Mac lunged at Raina, and his front foot slid out from underneath him on the mud. His arms windmilled, and he regained his balance. He spun around and scowled at Raina as if it was all her fault for the slippery ground.

Raina got on hands and knees and crawled, the mud squishing between her fingers. The roar of the falling rain and the gurgling ravine drowned out her racing heart. And icy droplets beat down on her, marking her slow progress. No one would hear her cry for help. One big shove, and she could tumble down to the ravine. No one would even find her body.

Big Mac grabbed hold of her ankle and yanked.

Raina flopped down onto her stomach. She twisted and kicked at him with the other foot. Didn't a knee injury end his basketball career? When he didn't let go, she turned and whacked her purse on his knee, over and over again. The walkie-talkie, cell phone, and other stuff turned her purse into an effective club.

Big Mac tried to keep his balance, but to no avail. He slid on the mud, letting go of Raina's ankle. She scrambled out of his way. He fell, slamming down on his side. Something popped. He yelped in pain, grabbing hold of his knee.

A clump of ferns rustled in the corner of Raina's eye, and she flinched. A flock of wild chickens burst from the fern grove. Both Raina and Big Mac swiveled their heads to look at the disturbance.

Out strolled Detective Mars and a uniform officer. Detective Mars brushed at his shoulders and grumbled to himself about spiders. When he finally noticed Raina and Big Mac covered with mud on the ground, his jaw dropped. "I don't even want to know why the two of you are wrestling in the mud. Which way to Leilani's apartment? We got lost following the path."

"Big Mac killed my cousin," Raina shouted. "And he's trying to get rid of me and Jenny Harris."

Detective Mars flicked a glance at Big Mac and back at Raina again. Several emotions crossed his face —the main one being whether he should let things take its course.

The uniformed officer watched his boss as if waiting for direction.

Big Mac got up slowly and winced when he put weight on his left leg. "I walked in on Raina trying to kill Jenny Harris. She is trying to avenge her cousin."

Detective Mars's gaze shifted to the motionless woman on the ground. "We can sort this out at the station." He pulled his cell phone out of his pocket and tapped on the screen, probably to call for backup.

Big Mac hobbled in the direction of the resort. "I'm heading back to the lobby and out of this rain. I will wait for you there."

Raina pointed at Big Mac's retreating back. "Go after him. Don't let him leave the resort. I have proof that he killed my cousin."

Detective Mars turned to the uniform officer. "You go after the perp"—he jerked a thumb at Raina's direction—"I'll stay here with her."

The uniformed officer took off after Big Mac, who had disappeared from view. For someone with an injured knee, the bartender moved like a bullet train.

Once the uniform officer was out of sight, Detective Mars raised an eyebrow at Raina. "The panda charm?"

Raina got up slowly from the ground, cold mud oozing between her toes. There was something disgraceful about being barefooted in front of the police, even if he was on the take. Should she pretend to be ignorant about the data on the panda charm, or should she press for a confession? Hopefully, the digital recorder app on her phone was still doing its job.

"I know about the data in the panda charm," Raina said, looking him dead in the eyes.

Detective Mars's expression didn't change, but the color drained from his face. He didn't say anything more, but he didn't have to. He smiled a crooked, nasty smile. "It looks like you're about to resist arrest and fall to your death in the ravine."

As he took a step toward Raina, pulling his handcuffs from his jacket pocket. A faint pop filled the air, just slightly louder than the pelting rain. And Detective Mars's eyes widened, and he sank to the ground, stiff as a board.

Ailani stepped out from behind him, holding onto Po Po's bright-red Taser. She tossed the pair of handcuffs at Raina. "Cuff him."

Raina scrambled behind Detective Mars to secure his hands behind his back. His eyes fluttered open. One of his irises was dilated, and the white part of the eye was completely red.

Ailani crouched beside the fallen detective and pressed her fingers to his neck. "He'll be okay in a minute."

Raina joined Ailani in facing the detective as he lay on the ground, trying to blink his red eyes. "What are you doing here?"

"After I read your note, I grabbed my Taser to find you at the resort," Ailani said. "You just missed me. I went downstairs to get my clothes from the dryer. I don't know what's going on, but I definitely had to step in. I can't let him hurt you. You're family."

"The red Taser belonged to Po Po. She lost it a few days ago in the rainforest," Raina said. She sank down onto the ground, not caring about the mud squishing onto places where the moon didn't shine. It wasn't like she could get any dirtier. "Thanks for believing in me, Ailani."

Her cousin gaped at Raina. "You knew I was pretending to be Leilani all this time?"

Detective Mars jerked and swiveled his gaze to Ailani. "Why? I thought we had a good thing going?"

"Yeah, right." Ailani snorted. "You might have a good thing going. I just wanted to get out. Bookkeeping for the triad is not exactly a career aspiration."

The detective glared at Ailani. The look of betrayal on his face looked almost comedic.

"I also know that Timothy Mars wants your panda charm and the data in it," Raina said. "Can you call nine-one-one?" She pulled out her cell phone to turn off the digital recorder app and emailed a copy of the audio file to her husband and grandma.

Matthew, Win, and a few male resort staff arrived shortly after. When Raina saw her husband, she squealed with happiness and jumped into his arms. Win knelt down next to Jenny, his hands shaking as he reached out to touch her face. Raina's heart ached for her brother.

After that, it was pandemonium. The uniform officer came back with a handcuffed Big Mac. Then more police officers arrived to take control of the scene. Many of them watched Detective Mars from the corner of their eyes, as if expecting a reprimand from a senior officer. The emergency medical technicians got Jenny into a gurney, and Win trotted beside them as they rushed back to the parked ambulance at the resort.

Raina wrapped both arms around Matthew's waist and watched the handcuffed Detective Mars and Big Mac hauled off to the police station. She beamed at Ailani, happy at the sight. The nightmare was finally over.

22

ROMANTIC HONEYMOON

After the police left, everyone assembled at the Wayfarer restaurant for a quick meal of deli sandwiches. Auntie May and Ailani disappeared into the resort office. When they came back an hour later, their faces were tear streaked, but there was an air of relief between them.

Matthew took the panda charm from Po Po and left the resort, probably to meet with Sonny Kwan and the feds. Po Po and Auntie May went to check on the damages at the honeymoon suite. And Raina found herself alone with Ailani at the tiki bar, watching the sunset on the beach beyond the underground imu. The rain had stopped, and the sky was a golden yellow and deep magenta. If it wasn't for the bruises on Raina's legs, she could almost believe what happened in the rainforest was a dream.

"I wondered when we'd get the chance to chat,"

Ailani said. She reached under the bar and pulled out two cans of Hawaiian Sun iced tea. She handed one to Raina and popped the top on her can. "You probably want to know why I pretended to be my sister."

Raina nodded. "That's not something people usually do unless they're up to some kind of mischief."

"I admit, it was a stupid idea. I regretted it the moment I was alone with my grandma. At the time, I thought it would buy me some time to make arrangements to leave the island. I had the money to start over, but I didn't want Timothy Mars to come after me."

"You could have compromised the entire investigation. Didn't you want justice for your sister's death?"

Ailani shrugged. "Not as much as I want my freedom back. When you work for a criminal organization like the Nine Dragons, a person can't simply quit. You leave the job through death."

Raina frowned, considering what Ailani had said. It didn't make sense for Auntie May to mix up the identity of the twins at the morgue. "Auntie May purposely claimed you were the victim to give you an opportunity to leave the Nine Dragons. She was hoping to buy you time."

Tears filled Ailani's eyes, and she blinked rapidly, hoping to hide them. "My grandma"—her voice came out in a croak, and she cleared her throat—"my grandma knew I wasn't Leilani?"

"Probably. Auntie May raised you and your sister, and I don't think she would make that kind of mistake.

Why are you at the resort? Why didn't you take the money and run?"

"Leilani called me after I picked up the ransom money. I'm used to the yelling, but she suddenly started slurring her words and stopped talking. I was still on the phone, and I heard a door slam and the phone hit the pavement. I got concerned. I wanted to make sure my sister was okay. I used the spare key to get into Leilani's apartment, but I must have fallen asleep while waiting for her. Then, the next morning, you showed up."

Goosebumps popped up on Raina's forearms. It felt as if someone walked over her grave. Ailani must have heard Leilani collapsing outside by the side door of the bar and knew instinctively that she needed to come to her sister's aid. "Are you still planning to leave now?"

"I don't know. The Nine Dragons won't let me off that easily. And I can't fill my sister's shoes."

"Timothy Mars will be behind bars. You can start over again."

"Just because the local crime boss is gone, doesn't mean they won't send somebody else to replace him. Sometimes all it takes is one wrong decision, and your entire life is over."

Raina shook her head. "Don't worry about the Nine Dragons. Matthew will take care of it." While she wouldn't consider Sonny Kwan a friend, they were still allies of a sort. "You just need to focus on helping

Auntie May get through this and take care of the resort."

Ailani studied Raina for a long moment, doubt in her eyes. "Is this similar to what the Ladies Justice Club does to help people?"

Raina blinked at the question. She had heard about the club in passing years ago. Wasn't her mom a club member? And what did a club in San Francisco have to do with things here? "I don't know anything about this club."

"I thought your grandma was a founding member."

Raina shrugged. Her grandma liked code names and secret clubs. It was hard to keep track of it all. "Matthew has connections. He can get the organization to forget that you even existed."

Ailani smiled and surprised Raina with a hug. "I guess we're going to be more than family. We can be friends."

A FEW DAYS LATER, Raina glanced across the candlelit table at her husband. They were seated on an outdoor patio of a fancy steakhouse by the beach. The waves crashed at the piers underneath the deck. The humid, salty air turned her curly, black hair into a frizz ball, but she didn't care. They were alone and dining at a nice restaurant that required Matthew to wear a jacket. The hubbub of conversation from the other diners and the scraping of utensils on plates created a romantic atmosphere.

While Raina was flying home tomorrow afternoon, her husband was staying behind. Tonight was their last chance to capture some semblance of a romantic honeymoon.

Their order arrived, and the server slid the plates in front of them. Steak and potatoes for Matthew. Surf and turf for Raina. The server left their table.

Matthew raised his glass of champagne—another unexpected extravagance. "To the perfect honeymoon."

Raina burst out laughing. Her husband was right. A murder investigation, an illegal gambling ring, and taking down a corrupted police department were the perfect honeymoon. "To us. For never having a dull moment."

They clinked glasses and drank.

"Good thinking about preserving the evidence in the broken cocktail glass," Matthew said. "It confirmed there was Rohypnol in Leilani's drink."

After the shakeup with the local police department, the state had asked the feds to step in, and Matthew became a consultant for the team. Her husband would stay behind for another week.

"What was Big Mac's reaction when he found out Ailani was the driver that night?" Raina said.

Matthew blinked at Raina in confusion. "I don't

think anyone has told him. Besides, do you think he needs to know?"

Raina put a piece of lobster in her mouth and chewed thoughtfully for a few seconds. Finally, she swallowed and said, "I see your point. I want to think that he regrets his actions and spends the rest of his life doing good deeds to redeem himself, but this probably won't happen. If he ever gets out on parole in the future, we don't want him coming after Ailani."

"How's Win doing?" Matthew asked, slicing into his steak.

Raina shrugged. Win had flown back home the day after Jenny Harris's arrest, leaving Po Po behind to help at the resort. "Mom said he is attending his college classes and working like usual. He isn't as happy-go-lucky as before, but I think he'll be okay. It pains me to see him hurt, but I guess that's how you grow up."

The corner of Mattie's lip twitched. "He's not a kid anymore. Stop going into parent mode on him. He's too polite to say it, but I'm sure it's irritating at times."

Raina bristled at the comment. "I am just a caring older sister."

"I know, Rainy, but why don't you save this for our kids?"

Raina's jaw dropped, forgetting about her momentary irritation.

Matthew chuckled at his wife's expression. "You win, honey. If it's up to me, we need more planning. But I have learned to trust your instinct. If you want to start a family now, then let's get on with it." He raised an eyebrow. "Maybe we can even practice tonight."

Raina glanced down at her dinner, feeling the heat rise on her cheeks. Even after all this time, he had a way of making her feel like a sappy love-struck teenager.

"And we can go car shopping when I get home," Matthew continued. There was no mistaking the pride in his voice. The Asian male provider struck again.

"What's wrong with my car?"

"It's time to replace it. Don't you want a newer car to drive the kids in? You won't want to get stranded on the side road with an infant."

"I'm not even pregnant yet. Aren't we jumping the gun a bit?"

"Replacing your car will not erase your father's memory."

Raina blinked at her husband. She didn't want to spoil the mood by getting into an argument, so she would let it slide for now. But she wasn't giving up her dad's car. Once it stopped running, it could become a lawn decoration as far as she was concerned.

At the next table, someone started clapping. Raina reached for her champagne glass and glanced over at the table. Po Po was giving her two thumbs up. Raina knocked over the champagne glass, spilling the drink across the tablecloth.

Po Po stood up with hands in the air and shouted, "I'm going to be a great granny again. Woohoo!"

Raina swiveled her gaze back to her husband. She glanced around at their table. Where was the bug? She lifted the bottle of steak sauce. No. Not under here.

Matthew pulled a small, black device out of his pocket and pressed a button on it. "It's an audio jammer. I don't know where your grandma is getting her spy toys, but she's creeping me out."

Raina snorted. "Tell me about it." She grabbed a napkin and started cleaning up the spilled wine on the table. When she glanced over at her grandma again, Po Po lifted her glass of wine in response and blew Raina a kiss.

"We better ask the front desk to move us to a different room," Matthew said. "We don't want your grandma to knock on the door when we're in the middle of making that great-grandchild."

THE END

Meet Lucy Fong
Just Shoot Me Dead
(Lucy Fong Mystery #1)

Meet Cedar Woods
Arrest the Allies
(Cedar Woods Mystery #1)

Get Anne R. Tan's FREE eBook Starter Library at http://annertan.com/newsletter

AUTHOR'S NOTE

I have always wanted to set a book in Kauai because of the wild chickens. My husband and I enjoyed a baby-moon there for my first pregnancy more than a decade ago. Unlike the other Hawaiian Islands, there is a wild chicken population on Kauai that rivals the pigeon count in some cities. Everywhere we went—from the open-air mall, the beach, the stores, and the resort—there was a flock of wild chickens. They just popped out from the vegetation at the oddest places. They pecked at the ground and got under people's feet without a care in the world. Of course, the locals on the island are used to it, but for a city person, I thought it was the most charming sight. I hope you enjoyed your time with the fictional wild chickens in this book.

And as always, thank you for supporting my art,
—Anne R. Tan

ACKNOWLEDGMENTS

A story is a dream that a writer brings to life on paper. But a book needs a team to nurture it into the enjoyable tale you've just read.

I want to thank my editors, Alicia S. and Adam, for wrangling my words so they are coherent.

And then, there are my wonderful beta-readers—Joyce S., Cindy I., Della D., Susan J., and Debi P.—thank you, ladies, for volunteering your time to catch these sneaky typos and grammatical errors.

And finally, thank you, Susan C. for the awesome cover.

I wouldn't have been able to bring this story to life without all of you, wonderful ladies. Thank you!

—Anne R. Tan

ALSO BY ANNE R. TAN

Thanks for reading *Airy Allies and Enemies.* I hope you enjoyed it!

Did you like this book?

Please review my books at your *retailer.* As an indie author, reviews help other readers find my books. I appreciate all reviews, whether positive or negative.

Want to know about new releases, sale pricing, and exclusive content?

Sign up for Anne R. Tan's Readers Club newsletter at http://annertan.com/newsletter

Your information would not be sold or transferred. Thank you for trusting me with your email.

Want More Raina Sun?

Raining Men and Corpses (Raina Sun #1)

Gusty Lovers and Cadavers (Raina Sun #2)

Breezy Friends and Bodies (Raina Sun #3)

Balmy Darlings and Death (Raina Sun #4)

Sunny Mates and Murders (Raina Sun #5)

Murky Passions and Scandals (Raina Sun #6)

Smoldering Flames and Secrets (Raina Sun #7)

Hazy Grooms and Homicides (Raina Sun #8)

Chilly Comforts and Disasters (Raina Sun #9)

Fair Cronies and Felonies (Raina Sun #10)

Airy Allies and Enemies (Raina Sun #11)

How about another series by Anne R. Tan?

Just Shoot Me Dead (Lucy Fong #1)

Just Lost and Found (Lucy Fong #1.5)

Just a Lucky Break-In (Lucy Fong #2)

JUST SHOOT ME DEAD

As the trill of the seldom-used ring tone filled the air, Lucy Fong jerked in her seat like someone had stabbed her rear with a needle, and the dumpling squirted out of her chopsticks, smacking into her date's glasses. It slid down his shirt before disappearing under the table, leaving a trail of grease and disappointment in its wake. She closed her eyes, wishing for a wormhole to open up beneath her feet.

In the last sixteen years, her estranged mother had only called her once, and that was when Lucy's stepfather had died. What bad news heralded the call this time? If it were good news, her half-sister would have posted it on social media by now. The conversation in the Chinese restaurant didn't miss a beat, and the clatter of eating utensils scraped against plates continued unabashed. Lucy's world had tilted on its axis, and no one had noticed.

Lucy opened her eyes, smiling like Miss America on steroids. "Sorry. At least it wasn't red wine." She was supposed to have dinner with just her grandma this evening but had accepted the extra dinner companions —a nice Chinese doctor and his mama—with grace. This wasn't the first set-up, but it would be the last. Her cell phone vibrated to indicate Mom had left a voicemail.

"I've gotten a drink thrown in my face, but never a dumpling." The doctor wiped his glasses, smearing the grease across the lens. "I'm always up for new experiences."

Lucy's smile wobbled. Ah, a man with a sense of humor. A rare commodity these days. Too bad this was like everything else in her life—the timing was off. She was still working with her therapist to fix the clock. "It must be rewarding to save people every day."

"I don't help people because it's rewarding. I help people because it's the right thing to do," the doctor said, sounding like he believed every word.

Lucy groaned inwardly. A do-gooder. He was definitely too good for the likes of her. She wasn't a "bad girl" by any stretch, but she certainly wasn't an ideal wife for a Chinese doctor from a long line of Chinese doctors. She snorted. She pitied the poor woman who did meet those ideals.

The doctor's mama scowled at Lucy. She probably wanted a nice Chinese girl for her precious boy and got a half-Chinese girl instead. The woman had insisted on speaking in Cantonese during the entire meal and giving Po Po pointed looks whenever Lucy stumbled over the words with her thick American accent. "I guess you're not much use in the kitchen if you can't even handle chopsticks."

"Lucy is an internet whizbang. Maybe she could help advertise your son's business?" Po Po said.

The doctor's mama stiffened. "That wouldn't be necessary."

Lucy wanted to slap money on the table for the meal and walk out the door. She didn't need this after a full week of work. But her grandma was all the family she had left...or all the family she wanted in her life. She glanced at Po Po, and the hopeful look on her grandma's face fizzled out.

Po Po filled the awkward silence with chatter about a murder investigation. Her grandma had recently cut off her long silver braid to favor a short pixie cut with pink streaks much like Lucy's. When Po Po got to the car chase in her story, Lucy tuned her out. Her grandma read too many mystery books as far as Lucy was concerned. The matriarch of the Wong family should have been Irish for all the gab she spun.

Lucy snorted, earning another dark look from the doctor's mama. Speaking of mothers, she better see what Mom wanted.

"Sorry, I need to take this call. It's from my mother," Lucy said, pushing back her chair.

Po Po's eyes widened with concern, and she bit her

lower lip as if to stop herself from saying something. She knew all about Lucy's tenuous relationship with her mother and half-sister.

"It's fine. We're done here," the doctor's mom said, dabbing at her lips with the cloth napkin.

Lucy thanked the doctor for a lovely dinner and shifted her gaze to Po Po. "I'll wait for you outside." She stumbled out of the restaurant, her heart pounding at the rejection from the doctor's family and the bruise to her ego.

The fog snaked around the red lanterns hung on the streets for the Chinatown tourists. Lucy shivered, but not from the chilly November night. Her hands shook when she pulled her cell phone from her purse. She tapped on the screen to listen to the voicemail, but instead of Mom's voice, the caller identified herself as Cousin Estelle.

YOUR MOTHER IS IN THE HOSPITAL. A NEIGHBOR FOUND HER SHOT IN THE STOMACH AT HER PRIVATE INVESTIGATION OFFICE. LUCY DEAR, YOU NEED TO COME HOME.

Her hands became numb, and the cell phone slipped onto the sidewalk. This couldn't be happening...

From behind her, she heard Po Po say goodnight to their dinner companions. Lucy swallowed the urge to throw up. Hurling the dumplings on the sidewalk would kill her reputation. The doctor's mama would make sure everyone knew Po Po's granddaughter was either a drunk or drug addict. San Francisco might be a big city, but Chinatown was a small community.

"Are you okay? What did your mother want?" Po Po said, rubbing Lucy's hunched back.

"It was her cousin. Mom is in the hospital," Lucy whispered, swallowing at the catch in her voice.

Po Po's lined face closed in like a flower petal. "Let's get you home, so you can pack to leave in the morning." She scooped up the cell phone and its battery off the sidewalk. "Broken. Why am I not surprised?" She tucked the phone into her purse. "Lucky you. I have a spare prepaid phone."

They strolled toward the brick three-story building two blocks away. The first floor housed the Fong Chinese Herbal Shop that once belonged to Lucy's deceased uncle. His apprentice ran the shop for her now. They got into the elevator, and Po Po hit the button for the third floor.

The keys rattled in Lucy's hand, and it took her three tries before she could open the door to her small apartment. She had lost a bedroom in the elevator renovation for the building, but it had been worth it. Her uncle had stayed in his home in the apartment across the hall until the end six months ago.

Once inside her small apartment, Po Po bustled around making tea in the plain terra cotta set her uncle had given her. The little ritual seemed out of place, given the gravity of the news, but comforting at the same time. Her uncle had done the same ritual when Lucy had shown up on his doorstep as a teenager in the middle of the night.

She glanced at the lucky cat clock on the wall with its plastic swaying tail. Eight thirty. If she left now, she might make it to the hospital by one in the morning. She glanced out the window. The thick fog hid the building next door, except for one speck of glow that might have been a window. Maybe it would be closer to two in the morning by the time she rolled into Morro Cliff Village, a small coastal hamlet on the Central Coast.

It would make more sense to leave in the morning and be much safer for a woman traveling alone. But what if Mom didn't make it through the night? Though they no longer had a close mother-daughter relationship, they once did. She blinked at the tears burning in the back of her eyes. She was going to be too late...

Po Po wrapped Lucy's hands around a steaming cup of tea. "It's only too late when you give up. We can swing by my house on the way out of the City. I can pack a bag in less than ten minutes."

When Lucy's late uncle had taken her in, this generous woman had claimed Lucy as one of her own, welcoming the angry teen into the Wong family all those years ago. She would do anything for this woman, but this wasn't the kind of road trip for Po Po to tag along.

"I want to go alone. I need the time to think," Lucy said.

"You can't drive like this. You're still in shock," Po Po said.

Lucy shook her head. "I'm fine. It's just...I thought there would be more time."

The fluorescent lights flickered overhead, casting a sick gray pallor over the hospital room despite the cheerful yellow walls. The lights were dim, and the room was only big enough to hold the hospital bed and chair. On the wall opposite the entrance was a tall and narrow window like the kind found in a medieval castle and a door that led to the bathroom. The only sounds in the room were the beeping and whirring machines that kept Mom alive.

Lucy stood with her hands tucked under her armpits at the footboard of the hospital bed, mesmerized by her mother's still form. She didn't recognize the woman in front of her. The mother in Lucy's memory was a tall and willowy woman with thick blonde hair. Lucy had inherited her Chinese father's black hair and the Fong family's love for pastries. She considered it a small miracle she still had the metabolism of her youth.

Mom had teased Lucy for being such a serious and reserved child. Whereas, Mom had been a vibrant woman, expressive and passionate, using her entire body when she moved or spoke. Or at least she did years ago. The elderly woman in front of Lucy had a permanent frown in her rail yard of a face. Her body was more shrunken than lush, and the blonde had become a mane of white. The years since her stepfather's death had been hard on Mom, and it showed.

Lucy willed herself to feel something, but there was nothing. The long drive in the dark had shuffled the fear into a corner. There was no sadness, no pain. Sure, Mom had chosen her husband and half-sister over Lucy, but that was a long time ago. Water under the bridge according to her therapist. And the anger had disappeared when her stepfather had died.

She just felt tired...and numb. Before the clumsy blind date, it had been a long day in the office, and her manager had screamed at Lucy for a data entry typo from a co-worker who was still on probation. Granted, as an internet marketing consultant, a single digit on a spreadsheet could kill an ad campaign, but it wasn't a gunshot wound.

Cousin Estelle slept awkwardly on the chair in the corner, her head leaning against the wall. She was actually her mom's younger cousin and in her mid-fifties. She had been a slender woman with too big front teeth and large ears when Lucy had left town. She had also been the unlucky recipient to inherit Great-grandma's first name. While she couldn't do anything with her teeth, her long dyed blonde hair hid the ears. Unfortunately, she had also grown in girth to match them.

Estelle jerked in her sleep and caught herself in time to keep from falling off the chair. She rubbed her sleepy hazel eyes and blinked at Lucy. She paused as if movement might make Lucy disappear.

"Thanks for calling me," Lucy whispered.

Estelle leapt off the chair and swept Lucy into a hug. Like the rest of the women in the Faye's side of the family, Estelle towered over Lucy at close to six feet tall. "It's so good to see you again." She pulled away, studying Lucy from head to toe. "Wow, you've grown into a little cutie pie."

Lucy raised an eyebrow. Little? In Chinatown, she had been as tall as most of the Chinese men at five foot six. She shook the random thoughts from her head. She wasn't here for a homecoming. "What happened?"

"I told you everything I know. You might want to talk to Max DeWitt later this morning. He's the town police chief now," Estelle said.

Lucy blinked. The last name DeWitt sounded familiar, and obviously, Estelle believed Lucy should remember him. "Did you talk to the doctor?"

Estelle shook her head. "Max tracked me down after your mom came out of surgery. The doctor makes his rounds in the morning around nine or ten. The nurse said your mother's condition is stable."

Lucy exhaled in relief. Stable sounded good. Maybe Mom would be back on her feet in a day or two, and Lucy could go home. "I can stay here if you want to go home."

Estelle held out a set of keys. "Why don't you go home and get some sleep? You have a long day ahead of you. I can't find your sister, and there wasn't anyone else..." She took a deep breath. "Do you want me to call a cleaning service for the office?" The words tumbled out in a nervous rush.

Lucy stiffened, trying to stop the shiver down her spine at the mention of the private investigation office. How much blood... She slammed a lid on the thought. "I'll deal with it later. Let me give you the number to my prepaid phone. It's a temporary loaner." She dug in her purse and came up with a receipt. She wrote down the number for her grandma's spare cell phone.

Estelle tucked the slip of paper into her bag. "After you settle in, maybe we can have dinner or..."

Lucy grabbed the spare keys and stumbled toward the door. Settle in? She wasn't staying. "Thank you for everything," she said over her shoulder. She couldn't stand another minute of the whirling machines.

In her haste, Lucy didn't see the man on the other side of the threshold. She stepped on his toe, and her head rammed into his chest. She would have fallen if he hadn't grabbed onto her forearms.

When Lucy straightened, she suppressed a sigh. Could this day get any worse?

"Max," Estelle said. Her voice brightened at his

appearance. "This is Lucy Fong, Dahlia Faye's...uh...daughter."

Lucy ground her teeth. Estelle was about to say *bastard daughter*. She couldn't believe people still remembered—or cared—that she was born out of wedlock. She shouldn't have come back. There wasn't anything she could do for her mother. She would only get insulted and shunned as she did in her childhood for being different. For having black hair among those with blonde or brown hair. For having slightly slanted eyes—

"Miss Fong, can I get you some coffee or tea?" Max DeWitt asked, his face concerned. "You seem to be in shock."

Lucy shook off his hands. "I'm fine. I need to go." Edging around Estelle and Max, she backed out of the room. Neither of them moved to stop Lucy, but she ran like the past might catch up with her.

The drive to Mom's three-bedroom Cape Cod house was a blur. One moment, Lucy was backing out of the parking spot of the hospital, and the next she was on the gravel path in front of the house, breathing in the salt air. She couldn't remember if she blew through stop signs or sped through the small waterfront down-town area. It was a good thing the shops weren't open for business yet.

When Lucy opened the front door to let herself in, her hands shook and jiggled the keys. It had to be from hunger. She refused to believe a woman she hadn't seen for over a decade would have this kind of impact on her. After all, the phone call from Estelle had interrupted dinner. After she checked in the attic bedroom, she would fish out the granola bar in her purse.

As she made her way up the stairs, Lucy caught glimpses of the ocean through the windows. The pale moonlight sparkled over the dark water. Though the ocean was tranquil from this angle, she knew it crashed against the rocks below the cliff.

Her steps thudded loudly in the silent house. For a moment, as the door to her old attic bedroom swung open, Lucy held her breath as if waiting for her half-sister to pop out from the closet. Of course, there was no chubby-cheeked preschooler. It had been sixteen years.

The room was just as she had left it—a twin bed against one wall, a desk next to a dormer window, and a small trunk against the far wall. The baseball bat was probably still underneath the bed. The posters of her teen idols curled on the edges, and the tape yellowed with age. Mom hadn't even cared enough to come up here to dust.

Continue Lucy's story.

Just Shoot Me Dead

ABOUT THE AUTHOR

Anne R. Tan is a *USA Today* bestselling author. She writes the Raina Sun Mystery series and the Lucy Fong Mystery series. Her humorous cozy mysteries feature Chinese-American amateur sleuths dealing with love, family, and life while solving murders.

Sign up for her newsletter for new release announcement, sales, and exclusive content at http://annertan.com/newsletter/

A NOTE FROM ANNE:

My books are my legacy to my children. Unfortunately, they won't grow up in the San Francisco Bay Area as I did. Without a cultural hub to keep the language and philosophies alive, our family will lose this part of our heritage in one generation. My children will be visitors to this rich culture just like my readers. I hope you'll enjoy your time with Raina Sun and her large dynamic family.